William Fearing Gill

The Life Of Edgar Allan Poe

William Fearing Gill

The Life Of Edgar Allan Poe

ISBN/EAN: 9783741134487

Manufactured in Europe, USA, Canada, Australia, Japa

Cover: Foto ©Raphael Reischuk / pixelio.de

Manufactured and distributed by brebook publishing software
(www.brebook.com)

William Fearing Gill

The Life Of Edgar Allan Poe

THE LIFE

OF

EDGAR ALLAN POE

BY

WILLIAM F. GILL

ILLUSTRATED

C. T. DILLINGHAM,
NEW YORK

CLAXTON, REMSEN & HAFFELFINGER
PHILADELPHIA

WILLIAM F. GILL & CO.
BOSTON

1877

GETCHELL BROS., PRS.,
252 Washington Street, Boston, Mass.

TO

NEILSON POE, ESQ.,

IN ACKNOWLEDGMENT OF THE KINDLY SYMPATHY AND VALUABLE AID
AFFORDED,

THIS VOLUME,

THE FIRST COMPLETE LIFE OF HIS KINSMAN, EDGAR ALLAN POE, YET
PUBLISHED,

IS RESPECTFULLY DEDICATED.

ERRATA.

In List of Illustrations, facing page 8, fifth line, "109" should be "131."

On page 142, fourteenth line, "dread " should be "terrors."

On page 143, tenth line, "has" should be "had."

On page 143, seventeenth line, "his attention" should be "himself."

PREFACE.

For more than a quarter of a century, the American public, while crowning with laurels the genius of Edgar A. Poe, has lived on, indolently oblivious of the true story of his life.

. Carping criticism has gloated over the doubtful record of follies and excesses ascribed to him by malignant enemies like Griswold, while the man, as he actually lived, is known only to the few.

But as truth gradually displaces falsehood, we shall come to understand more correctly the true proportions of that marred and broken individuality, that nature so sensitively organized and so rarely developed, under circumstances so exceptionally perilous and perverting.

Some years since, the attention of the writer of this memoir was called to numerous inconsistencies apparent in Dr. Rufus W. Griswold's memoir of Edgar Allan Poe, and was induced to make inquiries that evidenced that this memoir, which for twenty-five years has been permitted to stand as the representative biography of the poet, was, to all intents and purposes, a tissue of the most glaring falsehoods ever combined in a similar work.

It appeared, upon investigation, that Griswold's misrepresentations arose from the bitter enmity in which this mediocre writer held Poe, on account of the poet's slashing critique of his (Griswold's) "Poets and Poetry of America."

It has been the aim of the writer to give an unpartisan transcript of the life and character of Edgar Allan Poe; to be "to his faults a little kind," without shrinking from the duty of a biographer, to recount all facts that came within the scope of his province to record.

Place has not been given to idle rumors, nor to the unsubstantiated opinions of unreliable persons.

Dr. Griswold has been treated as a disagreeable necessity. So long as the impression created by his "memoir" exists, he cannot, in justice to the memory of the poet, be ignored on the ground of his mediocrity as a writer. IIis shafts were none the less pitiless, although barbed with "poor fustian." Until another quarter of a century has elapsed, it cannot be expected

that the baleful work done by Griswold can be up-
rooted, for it has stood and thriven during the past
twenty-five years, and, upon many persons now living, has created an impression that will endure while
life endures. To the new generation of readers, with
whom the lamented poet is finding a favor denied him
at the hands of his contemporaries, this memoir may
best fulfil its purpose of pleading the cause of a man
of genius, condemned unheard.

It may also serve to answer the complaint of an
English writer, that " no trustworthy biography of
of Poe has yet appeared in his own country."

It has been the design of the writer to include in
this work everything of importance that has been
written or related of Poe, so far as accessible and
reliable.

It has been our good fortune to be brought into
relations of near friendship with several of the most
intimate friends and companions of the poet; and in
many cases, we speak, literally, " out of their own
mouths," more significantly, without doubt, than if
we had had the temerity to assume more independent
views. Our especial acknowledgments, for valuable
assistance rendered, are due to Mrs. S. H. Whitman,

Mr. Neilson Poe, Mrs. Annie L. Richmond, Mr. George R. Graham, and the late Mrs. Maria Clemm and Mr. T. C. Clarke.

The portrait given is from a daguerrotype taken from life. It represents the poet in his youthful prime, and by one, a near friend of Poe, who has seen *all* his pictures known to be in existence, is pronounced the best likeness extant.

WILLIAM F. GILL.

CONTENTS.

CHAPTER I.
ANCESTRY.

CHAPTER II.
CHILDHOOD. 1809-1826.

CHAPTER III.
EARLY HARDSHIPS. 1826-1834.

CHAPTER IV.
BEGINNING A LITERARY CAREER. 1834-1838.

CHAPTER V.
VARIED EXPERIENCES IN PHILADELPHIA. 1838-1844.

CHAPTER VI.

CAREER IN NEW YORK. 1844-1846.

CHAPTER VII.

LAST YEARS. 1846-1849.

APPENDIX.

LIST OF ILLUSTRATIONS.

Poe's Cottage at Fordham, with vignettes suggested by his works.

THE LIFE
OF
EDGAR ALLAN POE.

CHAPTER I.
ANCESTRY.

The Origin of the Family Name, Italian — Founding of the
Race in Ireland — Family Feud with the Desmonds — Dis-
persion of the Families by Cromwell — Heroic Defence of
Don Isle — The Powers and Lady Blessington — General
David Poe — The Poet Counsellor — The Ballad of "Gra-
machree" — David Poe, Jr., and his Runaway Match —
Poe's Actress Mother — Convivial Southern Customs and
their Consequences — Place of Poe's Birth — Death of Poe's
Parents.

THE name Poe is an old Italian name,
and the minutest genealogical research
finds it antedating the river Po, which,
it is presumed, followed the original spelling of
the princely family from which it was named.
The family, like that of the Geraldines, and other
Anglo-Norman settlers in Ireland, passed from
Italy into the north of France, and from France,
through England and Wales, into Ireland, where,
from their isolated position and other causes, they
retained for a long period their hereditary traits,
with far less modification, from intermarriage and

consociation with other races, than did their English compeers.

Meantime, the name underwent various changes in accent and orthography.

We find descendants of the parent family rooted in Ireland as far back as 1327, the name in its Gallic form being spelled le Poer.

The disastrous civil war at this period, in which all the great barons of the country were involved, was occasioned by a personal feud between Arnold le Poer and Maurice of Desmond, the former having offended the dignity of the Desmond by calling him a rhymer.

We can well imagine that, sprung from a race to which the improvisation of poetry is a second nature, the sensitive ear of the le Poer could illy brook the ruder song of the untutored Celt.

Readers of the life of our poet will probably be impressed with the curious coincidence presented in his life-long battle with less cultured adversaries, with this contest of his Norman ancestor and his less gifted opponent. But the constitutional characteristics of the le Poers were at all times apparently distinguished by these marked combative elements, and as Mrs. Whitman remarks, in her admirable exposition of the literary career of Poe, "the possible influence, on a character so anomalous as that of Edgar Poe, of the mental and constitutional peculiarities of his ancestors, are certainly worthy of note."

During the reign of Henry II. of England, we find Sir Roger le Poer in Ireland, as Marshal to Prince John. Here he became the founder of a race connected with some of the most romantic and chivalrous incidents of Irish history.

The heroic daring of Arnold le Poer, Seneschal of Kilkenny Castle, who, we gather from Mrs. Whitman, interposed, at the ultimate sacrifice of his liberty and his life, to save a noble lady from an ecclesiastical trial for witchcraft, the first ever instituted in the kingdom, was chronicled by Geraldus Cambrensis, and has been commemorated by recent historians.

A transcript of the story, as told by Geraldus, may be found in Ennemoser's "Magic," and in White's "History of Sorcery."

The characteristics of the le Poers were marked and distinctive.

They were improvident, adventurous, and recklessly brave. They were deeply involved in the

Irish troubles of 1641; and when Cromwell invaded Ireland, he pursued them with a special and relentless animosity.

Their families were dispersed, their estates ravaged, and their lands forfeited.

Of the three leading branches of the family at the time of Cromwell's invasion, Kilmaedon, Don Isle, and Curraghmore, only the last escaped his vengeance. The present representative of Curraghmore is the Marquis of Waterford.

Cromwell's siege of the sea-girt castle and fortress of Don Isle, which was heroically defended by a female descendant of Nicholas le Poer, Baron of Don Isle, is, as represented by Sir Bernard Burke in his "Romance of the Aristocracy," full of legendary interest. The domain of Powerscourt took its name from the le Poers, and was for centuries in the possession of the family.

Lady Blessington, through her father, Edmond Power, claimed descent from the same old Norman family.*

A few branches of the family in Ireland still bore the old Italian name De la Poe, which, naturally, in its Anglicized form, became Poe.

----

* Illustrated London News, June 9, 1849.

John Poe, the great-grandfather of Edgar Allan Poe, married a daughter of Admiral McBride, distinguished for his naval achievements, and connected with some of the most illustrious families of England.

From genealogical records transmitted by him to his son David Poe, the grandfather of the poet, who was but two years of age when his parents left Ireland, it appears that different modes of spelling the name were adopted by different members of the same family.

David Poe was accustomed to speak of the Chevalier le Poer, a friend of the Marquis de Grammont, as having been of his father's family.

The grandfather of our poet was an officer in the Maryland line during the war of the Revolution, and an intimate friend of General LaFayette.

General Poe was, in the true sense of the word, a patriot. To furnish provisions, forage and clothing to the destitute government troops, he stripped himself of his entire patrimony. For this, he never instituted a claim, nor for services rendered to the United States as an officer; but for actual money loaned, he claimed forty thousand dollars. Owing to technical informalities in the vouchers

(which consisted principally of letters from
Washington and LaFayette), he received no portion of the sum. The Maryland legislature,
however, subsequently allowed his widow a pen-
sion, and, in the preamble of the act, expressed
their satisfaction of the *equity* of the claim, while
they deplored the *legal* insufficiency of the proofs
to support it. General Poe was one of the most
intimate personal friends of LaFayette, who, during his memorable visit to America in 1824,
called upon the widow, publicly acknowledged
the obligations of the country to her husband, expressed his astonishment at finding her in comparative indigence, and evinced his strong indignation at the narrow-minded policy of the government. We gather a few particulars of this
interview from the late "Baltimore Gazette," and
other papers of the time: "General LaFayette
affectionately embraced Mrs. Poe, exclaiming at
the same time, in tears, ' The last time I embraced
you, madame, you were younger and more
blooming than now.' He visited, with his staff,
the grave of General Poe, in 'the First Presbyterian Church-yard,' and kneeling on the ground,
kissed the sod above him, and, weeping, ex-

claimed, '*Ici repose un cœur noble!*'—here lies a noble heart!—a just tribute to the memory of a good, if not a great, man."

A relative of David Poe, belonging to the Irish branch, although a lawyer by profession, was, like his now famous descendant, possessed of the divine afflatus, and one of his ballads so fascinated Robert Burns, the Scottish poet, that he included it in a collection of Scottish songs and ballads, ancient and modern, which, with anecdotes of their authors, says Cunningham, exists in the handwriting of Burns in an interleaved copy of the first four volumes of Johnson's "Musical Museum," which the poet presented to Captain Riddel, of Friar's Corse.

We quote the beautiful ballad, with Burns' introductory comment:

"The song of 'Gramachree' was composed by Mr. Poe, a counsellor at law in Dublin. This anecdote I had from a gentleman who knew the lady, the 'Molly,' who is the subject of the song, and to whom Mr. Poe sent the first manuscript of these most beautiful verses.* I do not remember any single line that has more pathos than

-----

* Burns also apologized for placing an Irish poem in a

> " 'How can she break the honest heart
>   That wears her in its core!'"

As down on Banna's banks I stray'd,
   One evening in May,
The little birds in blithest notes
   Made vocal every spray;
They sang their little notes of love!
   They sang them o'er and o'er:
Ah! gramachree, mo challie nouge,
   Mo Molly Astore.

The daisy pied, and all the sweets
   The dawn of nature yields,
The primrose pale, the violet blue,
   Lay scatter'd o'er the fields;
Such fragrance in the bosom lies
   Of her whom I adore:
Ah! gramachree, mo challie nouge,
   Mo Molly Astore.

I laid me down upon a bank,
   Bewailing my sad fate,
That doom'd me thus the slave of love,
   And cruel Molly's hate.

---

collection in which it had no legitimate place. He evidently
wished to embalm Mr. Poe's exquisite verses in a permanent
form, and was willing, in his admiration of them, to disregard
the fitness of things.

How can she break the honest heart
   That wears her in its core!
Ah! gramachree, mo challie nouge,
   Mo Molly Astore.

You said you loved me, Molly dear:
   Ah! why did I believe?
Yes, who could think such tender **words**
   Were meant but to deceive?
That love was all I ask'd on earth,
   Nay, Heaven could give no more!
Ah! gramachree, mo challie nouge,
   Mo Molly Astore.

Oh! had I all the flocks that graze
   On yonder yellow hill,
Or low'd for me the num'rous herds
   That yon green pastures fill,
With her I love I'd gladly share
   My kine and fleecy store:
Ah! gramachree, mo challie nouge,
   Mo Molly Astore.

Two turtle doves, above my head,
   Sat courting on a bow;
I envy'd them their happiness,
   To see them bill and coo;
Such fondness once for me she show'd,
   But now, alas! 'tis o'er
Ah! gramachree, mo challie nouge,
   Mo Molly Astore.

> Then fare thee well, my Molly dear,
>   Thy loss I still shall moan;
> Whilst life remains in Strephon's heart,
>   'Twill beat for thee alone.
> Though thou art false, may Heaven on thee
>   Its choicest blessings pour!
> Ah! gramachree, mo challie nouge,
>   Mo Molly Astore.

General Poe married a Pennsylvania lady by the name of Cairnes, who is still remembered as having been a woman famous for her singular beauty. They had five children, of whom the fourth, David, was the father of the poet. The manners and customs prevailing among the better class of Southerners, at this period when David Poe, Jr., was growing into manhood, were little calculated to foster healthful moral restraints in the younger generation.

The punch-bowl was as indispensable a fixture in the hall as was the card-basket, and potations from the generous liquor were as freely and innocently indulged in as are draughts of ice-water at the present time. The custom probably came into vogue during the days of the Revolution, and doubtless answered well for campaigners, with irksome out-of-door duties. In the warm climate of the South its baleful effects soon came to be felt, but not until the manhood of many well-intentioned young men had been unwittingly sacrificed by the acquisition of a habit of drink quite beyond control. David Poe, Jr., not unnaturally, fell a victim to the indulgences of the flowing bowl, and manifested indications of a weakness which excited great solicitude among his family and friends.

While yet a law student in the office of William Gwynne, Esq., Baltimore, Maryland, he became enamoured with Elizabeth Arnold, a young English actress of considerable repute, and, at the age of eighteen, eloped with and married her.

His parents, with the reprehensible contempt for the stage which then obtained, and which, more is the pity, still obtains to a great degree, disowned the young man, and he was thrown upon his own resources. Naturally enough, he went upon the stage, supporting his wife in several of her engagements throughout the country, but, with his limited experience, never, of course, attaining any position of importance.

Upon the birth of their first child, William Henry Leonard Poe, a reconciliation between

him and his family was, according to some accounts, cemented; but we doubt if David Poe
returned to the paternal mansion, for Edgar was
born in Boston, while his mother was playing an
engagement there, and all accounts agree that
the couple remained upon the stage up to the
time of their death. Mrs. Poe died from pneu-
monia, during an engagement at the Richmond
Theatre, December 8, 1811.

In the files of the Richmond Enquirer of that
year, under date of December 10, is found the
following obituary notice:

"Died, on Sunday last, Mrs. Poe, one of the actresses of
the company now playing on the Richmond boards. By the
death of this lady the stage has been deprived of one of its
brightest ornaments, and, to say the least of her, she was an
interesting actress, and never failed to catch the applause and
command the admiration of the beholder."

Poe's father was one of the victims of the
burning of the Richmond Theatre on the 26th
of the same month in which Mrs. Poe died: *

Their three orphaned children, William Henry, Edgar, and Rosalie, all of tender years, were
left unprovided for, but the general sympathy
aroused at the time by the fire was extended to
them, and they were all well cared for by kind
friends.

* Some authorities state that Mr. Poe died of consumption,
two weeks after the death of his wife.

CHAPTER II

CHILDHOOD.

1809–1826.

Birth of the Poet — Early Beauty and Fascination — Poe's Foster Father — Precocious Predilection for the Muses — At School in England — Stoke Newington and Rev. Dr. Bransby — At School in Richmond — First Ideal Love — Death of Helen Stannard — First Volume of Juvenile Poems — At the University of Virginia — Testimony of the Faculty of the University — Morbid and Sensitive Temperament — Athletic Achievements.

EDGAR ALLAN POE was born in Boston, on the 19th of January, 1809.

Born to privation, marked before his birth with the brand of his father's vice, the orphan of two years seemed called upon to face an abject future. But a glamour of sunshine, at least, was destined to illume his path. It was but a glamour, a glamour that proved in the end but as a winding-sheet to the hopes of our poet. The extraordinary beauty and captivating manners of Edgar unfortunately won the attention of a gentleman residing in Richmond, Mr. John Allan, a man of wealth and position. We use

(21)

the word "unfortunately," advisedly, since the imaginative child must have received, among the first impressions of his new home, the idea of the great inheritance to which he was to look forward, and have become at the outset sur-charged with the spirit of self-willed independence, which such anticipations were calculated to create and strengthen. Mr. Allan's income was princely, and as he had no children, there was no reserve in the admission that he designed his adopted son to be the inheritor of his fortune.

These were the poet's halcyon days; and even at this early time he evinced his predilection for the muses. Mr. Stoddard tells us that he was remarkable for a tenacious memory and a musical ear, and that he was accustomed to declaim the finest passages of English poetry to the evening visitors at Mr. Allan's house, with great effect. The most insensible of his audience could not fail to be struck with the justness of his emphasis, and his evident appreciation of the poems he recited, while every heart was won by the ingenuous simplicity and agreeable manners of the precocious elocutionist.

In 1817, Mr. and Mrs. Allan paid a lengthened visit to England, being concerned in the disposal of some property there. Edgar, now Edgar Allan, after his adopted father, accompanied them, and was placed in charge of the Rev. John Bransby, at Stoke Newington.

Poe's partly autobiographical description of this school at Stoke Newington is found in one of his matchless short stories, "William Wilson:"—

"My earliest recollections of a school life are connected with a large, rambling Elizabethan house, in a misty-looking village of England, where were a vast number of gigantic and gnarled trees, and where all the houses were excessively ancient. In truth, it was a dream-like and spirit-soothing place, that venerable old town. At this moment, in fancy, I feel the refreshing chilliness of its deeply-shadowed avenues, inhale the fragrance of its thousand shrubberies, and thrill anew with undefinable delight, at the deep hollow note of the church bell, breaking, each hour, with sullen and sudden roar, upon the stillness of the dusky atmosphere in which the fretted Gothic steeple lay embedded and asleep. It gives me, perhaps, as much of pleasure as I can now in any manner experience, to dwell upon minute recollections of the school and its concerns. Steeped in misery as I am—misery, alas! only too real—I shall be pardoned for seeking relief, however slight and temporary, in the weakness of a few rambling details. These, moreover, utterly trivial and even ridiculous in themselves, assume, to my fancy, adventitious importance, as connected with a period and locality when and where I recognize the first ambiguous monitions of the destiny which afterward so fully overshadowed me. Let me then remember. The house, I have said, was old and irregular. The grounds were extensive, and a high and solid brick wall, topped with a bed of mortar and broken glass, encompassed the whole. The prison-like rampart formed the limit of our domain; beyond it we saw but thrice a week—once every Saturday afternoon, when, attended by two ushers, we were permitted to take brief walks in a body through some of the neighboring fields—and twice during Sunday, when we were paraded in the same formal manner to the morning and evening service in the one church of the village. Of this church the principal of our school was pastor. With how deep a spirit of wonder and

perplexity was I wont to regard him from our
remote pew in the gallery, as, with step solemn
and slow, he ascended the pulpit! This reverend man, with countenance so demurely benign,
with robes so glossy and so clerically flowing,
with wig so minutely powdered, so rigid and so
vast,—could this be he who, of late, with sour .
visage and in snuffy habiliments, administered,
ferule in hand, the Draconian laws of the academy? Oh, gigantic paradox, too utterly mon-
strous for solution! At an angle of the ponderous wall frowned a more ponderous gate. It was
riveted and studded with iron bolts, and surmounted with jagged iron spikes. What impressions of deep awe did it inspire! It was never
opened save for the three periodical egressions
and ingressions already mentioned; then, in
every creak of its mighty hinges, we found a
plenitude of mystery—a world of matter for solemn remark, or for more solemn meditation.
The extensive inclosure was irregular in form,
having many capacious recesses. Of these, three
or four of the largest constituted the playground.
It was level, and covered with fine hard gravel.
I well remember it had no trees, nor benches,

nor anything similar, within it. Of course it was in the rear of the house. In front lay a small parterre, planted with box and other shrubs; but through this sacred division we passed only upon rare occasions indeed—such as a first advent to school or final departure thence, or, perhaps, when a parent or friend having called for us, we joyfully took our way home for the Christmas or Midsummer holidays. But the house!—how quaint an old building was this!—to me how veritably a palace of enchantment! There was really no end to its windings—to its incomprehensible subdivisions. It was difficult, at any given time, to say with certainty upon which of its two stories one happened to be. From each room to every other there were sure to be found three or four steps either in ascent or descent. Then the lateral branches were innumerable—inconceivable—and so returning in upon themselves, that our most exact ideas in regard to the whole mansion were not very far different from those with which we pondered upon infinity. During the five years of my residence here, I was never able to ascertain with precision, in what remote locality lay the little

sleeping apartment assigned to myself and some
eighteen or twenty other scholars. The school-
room was the largest in the house — I could not
help thinking, in the world. It was very long,
narrow, and dismally low, with pointed Gothic
windows and a ceiling of oak. In a remote and
terror-inspiring angle was a square inclosure of
eight or ten feet, comprising the *sanctum*, 'during
hours,' of our principal, the Reverend Dr. Bransby. It was a solid structure, with massy door,
sooner than open which in the absence of the
'Dominie,' we would all have willingly perished
by the *peine forte et dure*. In other angles were
two other similar boxes, far less reverenced,
indeed, but still greatly matters of awe. One of
these was the pulpit of the 'classical' usher, one
of the 'English and mathematical.' Interspersed
about the room, crossing and recrossing in end-
less irregularity, were innumerable benches and
desks, black, ancient and time-worn, piled des-
perately with much-bethumbed books, and so
beseamed with initial letters, names at full length,
grotesque figures, and other multiplied efforts of
the knife, as to have entirely lost what little of
original form might have been their portion in

days long departed.   A huge bucket with water
stood at one extremity of the room, and a clock
of stupendous dimensions at the other.

"Encompassed by the massy walls of this venerable academy, I passed, yet not in tedium or
disgust, the years of the third lustrum of my life.
The teeming brain of childhood requires no ex-
ternal world of incident to occupy or amuse it;
and the apparently dismal monotony of a school
was replete with more intense excitement than
my riper youth has derived from luxury, or my
full manhood from crime.   Yet I must believe
that my first mental development had in it much
of the uncommon—even much of the *outre*.
Upon mankind at large the events of very early
existence rarely leave in mature age any definite
impression.   All is gray shadow—a weak and
irregular remembrance—an indistinct regathering of feeble pleasures and phantasmagoric pains.
With me this is not so.   In childhood I must
have felt with the energy of a man what I now
find stamped upon memory in lines as vivid, as
deep, and as durable as the *exergues* of the Car-
thaginian medals.   Yet the fact—in the fact of
the world's view—how little was there to remem-

Rev. Dr. Bransby's Establishment at Stoke-Newington.

The School Play-Ground at Stoke-Newington.

ber. The morning's awakening, the nightly
summons to bed; the connings, the recitations;
the periodical half-holidays and perambulations;
the playground, with its broils, its pastimes, its
intrigues; these, by a mental sorcery long forgotten, were made to involve a wilderness of
sensation, a world of rich incident, an universe
of varied emotion, of excitement the most passionate and spirit-stirring. '*O, le bon temps, que
ce siècle de fer!*'"

Poe, in his description of the school-house at
Stoke Newington, as in most of his pictures from
life, drew upon his imagination somewhat.

The actual house was identified a few years
ago by the late Mr. John Camden Hotten, the
London publisher. By a fortunate circumstance,
Mr. Hotten stumbled upon an abstract of the
leases granted by the Lord of the Manor, sixty
years since, and amongst the entries was found
the following : —

Yearly rent.

The Rev. John Bransby, of the school in Church
   street, and ground in Edwards lane, 21 years
   lease, with 10 additional, expires March, 1837 . £55.00

As Bransby was the name mentioned in the
story, this gave a clue, and the house was

soon identified, but not as having "Elizabethan gables."

The actual house is a roomy old structure, of Queen Anne's time, and remains internally in very nearly the same state as when Poe went to school there. It is a school at present, under the care of a Mr. Dod, and although the thirteen acres of playground, which existed in Poe's time, have long since been parcelled out to other tenements, or have been built upon, we were fortunate in being able to secure a good sketch of the house, together with a drawing, made whilst Poe was at the school, of the ancient manor gateway, formerly a conspicuous object in the ground.

The portrait of Poe's schoolmaster is interesting, when taken in connection with the poet's graphic description of the venerable clergyman in "William Wilson."

Returning from England, Poe was placed at school in Richmond for a short time, under Mr. Joseph Clarke, who is still living, at Baltimore.

According to Mrs. Whitman, one of the most accurate as well as one of the most accomplished of Poe's biographers, Poe was at this time twelve years of age.

THE REV. DR. BRANSBY.
(Poe's English Schoolmaster.)

Here the embryo poet experienced what he wrote of, in the last year of his life, as "the one idolatrous and purely ideal love of his passionate boyhood." As instancing a peculiar phase of Poe's character, his sad, remorseful pity for the departed, which, as Mrs. Whitman writes, is everywhere a distinguishing feature in his prose and poetry, this characteristic incident, which the lady describes in her monograph on Poe, affords a striking illustration.

One day, while at the academy at Richmond, he accompanied a schoolmate to his home, where he saw for the first time Mrs. Helen Stannard, the mother of his young friend.

This lady, on entering the room, took his hand and spoke some gentle, gracious words of welcome, which so penetrated the sensitive heart of the orphan boy as to deprive him of the power of speech, and, for a time, almost of consciousness itself.

He returned home in a dream, with but one thought, one hope in life : to hear again the sweet, gracious words of welcome that had made the desolate world so beautiful to him, and filled his lonely heart with the oppression of a new joy.

Mrs. Stannard afterwards became the confidant of all his boyish sorrows; and hers was the one redeeming influence that saved and guided him in the earlier days of his turbulent and passionate youth.

When she died, his grief was so boundless, that for months after her decease, he made nightly visits to the cemetery where the object of his boyish idolatry lay entombed.

His predisposition to loneliness and melancholy, found a welcome outlet here; and it was on the coldest and dreariest nights, when the autumnal rains fell, and winds wailed mournfully over the graves, that he lingered longest and came away most regretfully.

His boy-love for this lady was the inspiration of many of his exquisite creations. Her image, long and tenderly cherished, suggested the three exquisite stanzas to Helen* which first appeared in one of the earlier editions of his poetry, — stanzas

---

* Helen, of the poem entitled "The Pæan," which he subsequently re-wrote and greatly improved under the now familiar name "Lenore," was unquestionably Helen Stannard.

written in his youth, which James Russell Lowell
says have in them a grace and symmetry of outline such as few poets ever attain, and which are
valuable as displaying "what can only be expressed by the contradictory phrase of innate
experience."   •

"In 1822," says Dr. Griswold, "he entered the
university at Charlottesville, Virginia, where he
. led a very dissipated life. The manners which
then prevailed there were extremely dissolute,
and he was known as the wildest and most reckless student of his class; but his unusual opportunities, and the remarkable ease with which he
mastered the most difficult studies, kept him all
the while in the first rank for scholarship, and he
would have graduated with the highest honors,
had not his gambling, intemperance and other
vices induced his expulsion from the university."

This is all false from beginning to end, and is
absurd, likewise, on the biographer's own showing. If Poe was born in 1811, as 'Griswold
states, he would at this time (1822) have been
eleven years of age.   Rather a precocious age, is
it not, for one to whom is ascribed the rôle of a
rake and a gambler? As a matter of fact, Poe

did not enter the university until 1826, being then just seventeen years of age.

The testimony of Dr. S. Maupin, president of the University of Virginia, and of Mr. William Wertenbaker, the secretary, effectually refutes the mendacities of Poe's original biographer upon this point. Mr. Wertenbaker writes, —

"Edgar A. Poe was a student of the University of Virginia during the second session, which commenced February 1, 1826, and terminated December 15 of the same year. He signed the matriculation book on the 16th of February, and remained in good standing as a student till the session closed.

"He was born on the 19th of January, 1809, being a little under seventeen when he entered the institution. He belonged to the school of ancient and modern languages, and, as I was myself a member of the latter, I can testify that he was tolerably regular in attendance, and a very successful student, having obtained distinction in it in the final examination, — the highest a student could then obtain, the present regulation in regard to degrees not having been at the time adopted.

"On one occasion Prof. Batterman requested his Italian class to render into English verse a portion of the lesson in Tasso, assigned for the next lecture. Mr. Poe was the *only one* who complied with the request. He was highly complimented by the professor for his performance. Although I had a passing acquaintance with Mr. Poe from an early period of the session, it was not till near its close that I had any social intercourse with him.

"After spending an evening together at a private house, he invited me to his room. It was a cold night in December, and his fire having gone nearly out, by the aid of some candle ends and the wreck of a table he soon rekindled it, and by its comfortable blaze I spent a very pleasant hour with him. On this occasion he spoke with regret of the amount of money he had wasted, and the debts he had contracted.

"In a biographical sketch of Mr. Poe, I have seen it stated that he was at one time expelled from the university, but that he afterwards returned and graduated with the highest honors. This is entirely a mistake. He spent but one session at the university, and at no time did he fall under

the censure of the faculty.   He was not at that
time addicted to drinking, but had an ungovern-
able passion for card-playing.   Mr. Poe was older
than his biographer represents him.   His age, I
have no doubt, was correctly entered on the
matriculation book."

In a brief note accompanying the statement of
the secretary, Mr. Wertenbaker, the president
of the university, Mr. S. Maupin, writes, —

"Mr. Wertenbaker's statement is full upon all
the points specified, and is worthy of entire confidence.   I may add that there is nothing in the
faculty records to the prejudice of Mr. Poe.   ˉ

"He appears to have been a successful student,
having obtained distinctions in Latin and French
at the closing examination of 1826.   He never
formally graduated here, no provision for confer-
ring degrees of any kind having been made at
the time he was a student here."

In further confirmation of the correctness of
Mr. Wertenbaker's estimate of Poe at this time,
the following extracts from a manuscript letter,
written by a schoolmate, Mr. John Willis, of
Orange County, Virginia, may be cited:

"Poe had many noble qualities, and nature had endowed
him with more of genius, and a far greater diversity of talent,

than any other whom it had been my lot to have known. He had a fine talent for drawing, and the walls of his room at college were completely covered with his crayon sketches. His disposition was rather *retiring*, and he had few intimate associates. ·

. . . "I trust you will be able to collect enough to vindicate the character of Edgar Poe from every aspersion; for, whatever may have been the errors, the misfortunes or the frailties of his after-life, in the days of his youth, when first entering upon manhood, his bosom was warmed by sentiments of the most generous and noble character.

"Very respectfully yours,
"JOHN WILLIS."

That Poe's morbid, sensitive temperament did not predispose him to conviviality is, indeed, evidenced in some of his partly autobiographical stories. His affectionate disposition, indeed, found little response, either from his proud yet indulgent foster father, or from his youthful playmates; and it is evident, from reading his own description of his isolation at this time, as given in "The Black Cat," that he grew up self-ostracized from most of the usual associations with others that are common in childhood.

"From my infancy I was noted for the docility and humanity of my disposition. My tenderness of heart was even so conspicuous as to make me

the jest of my companions. I was especially
fond of animals, and was indulged by my parents with a great variety of pets. With these
I spent most of my time, and never was so happy
as when feeding and caressing them.

"This peculiarity grew with my growth, and
in my manhood I derived from it one of my principal sources of pleasure.

"To those who have cherished an affection for
a faithful and sagacious dog, I need hardly be at
the trouble of explaining the nature or the intensity of the gratification thus derivable.

"There is something in the unselfish and self-
sacrificing love of a brute, which goes directly to
the heart of him who has had frequent occasion
to test the paltry friendship and gossamer fidelity
of mere man."

Poe, however, was not a morbid recluse. In
these youthful days we find him emulating the
daring deeds of his Norman ancestors, in gym-
nastic feats, that, but for attested documentary
evidence, would scarcely be credited.

He was very proud of his athletic achievements,
as, indeed, he had good reason to be.

"At one period he was known to leap the dis-

tance of twenty-one feet six inches, on a dead
level, with a run of twenty yards. A most remarkable swim of his is also on record in the
columns of the 'Richmond Enquirer,' and other
Richmond papers. It took place in his fifteenth
year. He swam, on a hot July day, against a
three-knot tide, from Ludlam's wharf on James
River, to Warwick—a distance of seven miles
and a half,—fully equal to thirty miles in still
water. The impossibility of resting, even for a
moment, by floating, in a task such as this, renders it Herculean, and the feat has never been
equalled by any one, properly authenticated.

CHAPTER III.

1827 — 1834.

Home from School — First Quarrel with Mr. Allan — First
Meeting with Virginia Clemm — A Second Edition of Ju-
venile Poems — A Griswold Fabrication Disproved — Wil-
liam Henry Leonard Poe — Poe and the Milford Bard —
An Amusing Poetic Duel — Poe at West Point — A Third
Edition of Poems — The True Story of Poe's Dismissal
from West Point — Another Quarrel with Mr. Allan —
Second Marriage of Mr. Allan — Poe at Mrs. Clemm's —
A Lie Refuted — The Baltimore Prizes — Mr. J. H. B.
Latrobe's Account — Poe and Hewitt — Pen Photograph
of the Poet at 24 years — "Adventures of Hans Pfaal" — The
Heir Expectant Left Penniless.

RETURNING home after completing his
college career, Poe, like other spoiled
children of pampering fathers, found
that the fruits of the heedless indulgence in which
he had been reared, were not acceptable to his
foster father, when they came in the guise of
drafts given to pay gambling debts.

Mr. Allan declining to pay some of these
drafts, the high-spirited youth left the Allans'
house in high dudgeon, and took refuge, for the

(40)

time being, with his father's sister, Mrs. Maria Clemm.

Here he first saw his cousin Virginia, then a fairy-like child of six years. He naturally became interested in his pretty little relative, and undertook her education by way of occupation. About this time, he published a second edition of juvenile poems, his estrangement from his foster father and dependence upon his aunt having probably suggested the publication.*

Most authors are more sanguine as to the success of their first book than at a later period, when experience has taught them wisdom; and young Poe was, it is presumed, not an exception in this respect.

Griswold writes that Poe, after quitting the Allans at this time, left the country with the quixotic intention of joining the Greeks, then in the midst of their struggle with the Turks.

According to this unscrupulous writer, "he never reached his destination, and we know but little of his adventures in Europe for nearly a year.

---

* Hatch & Dunning, Baltimore, 1829.

"By the end of this time he had made his way to St. Petersburg, and our minister in that capitol, the late Mr. Henry Middleton, of South Carolina, was summoned one morning to save him from penalties incurred in a drunken debauch. Through Mr. Middleton's kindness, he was set at liberty and enabled to return to this country." Whether this is, like other statements from this source, a fabrication from beginning to end, or takes its color from a story told of an adventure of William Henry Poe, the brother of Edgar, cannot be determined. Certain it is, however, that our poet never set foot in Europe at all; his cousin, Mr. Neilson Poe, a prominent attorney, now residing in Baltimore, authorizing the statement, that to his positive knowledge Poe never left America at any time, although his brother did make a European trip.

This brother, William Henry Leonard Poe, was a young man of fine appearance, prepossessing countenance, and an intellectual forehead.

A phrenologist at a glance would pronounce his head a fine one, although the animal propensities greatly overbalanced the moral and intellectual.

He was à young man of irregular habits, of a sanguine temperament, and a poet of some promise. He died in early manhood. As it has been said, that, had he lived, he would have rivalled his more renowned brother, we give some specimens of his verse contributed to the "Minerva," a weekly paper conducted by Mr. J. H. Hewitt, of Baltimore:

TO ———.

A bitter tear for thee is shed,
   Friend of my soul, fair child of feeling!
The hopes that once existence fed,
Now live no more; the heart that bled
   For thee in self-contempt congealing.
Twine not for me a roseate wreath, —
   'T will wither on the brow of care;
But cull from the silent bed of death,
   Blossoms that flourish sadly there;
Sighs may expand their hour of bloom,
Tears make them glitter through the gloom,
   But oh! the light of smiles may blight
The tender blossoms of the tomb.

Go, and in fashion's plumage gay,
   Though it was won by years of sorrow,
Pluck care from out thy soul, and say,
"I'll wear the smile of joy to-day,
   Though anguish wring my heart to-morrow."

And with thee take my heart; 't is thine,
  Though guilty and too frail to trust;
While I, alone, unknown, shall pine
  And banquet on my soul's disgust.
Live, if thou canst, devoid of art,
Rich in pure tenderness of heart,
  And on thy way may Virtue's ray
With all its soft effulgence dart.

Farewell! thy face is clouded now,
  But soon a thousand smiles will flutter
Around thy lips, and that proud brow
Shall wear away the plighted vow
  Thy lying lips now softly utter.
Go, and a heaven of peace be thine,
  The fairest flowers the eye can find
Be on thy path; should mem'ry shine
  Upon the *friend* thou leavest behind,
Give to his fate a heartfelt tear,
But still let pleasure's sunshine peer
  Upon thy heart, where'er thou art, —
It will not make thy form less dear.

————

TO MINNIE.

The rose that gloried on your breast,
  And drew life from your glowing heart,
Has oft to mine been closely pressed,
  Too close, too fondly e'er to part.

Why did you spurn it from its home
  The sunshine of those sparkling eyes?
'Tis near my heart, yet will not bloom,
  But withers in my tears and sighs.

Although its perfume still remains,
  Yet every leaf conceals a thorn;
Just like the heart in sorrow's chains
  When every ray of hope is gone.

And like that rose, affection wears,
  At first, a tint as pure and gay,
Till 'neath the tide of worldly cares,
  Its smiles of beauty fade away.

But still behind it leaves a pain,
  A quick and penetrating smart,
The thorns of blasted hope remain,
  And pierce the sad and broken heart.

The publication of Poe's book of verses excited no especial public comment at the time of their issue.

There were, in fact, but two literary journals in Baltimore at this time, and the only paper that noticed the work critically, "The Minerva," handled it rather roughly. Many of the verses were crude to a degree, and the enterprise that has led to their recent republication, contrary to the expressed dictum of the poet, seems incomprehensible.

An amusing episode, connected with the career of the young poet at this time, is narrated by a Baltimore acquaintance of Poe. The "Milford Bard," who flourished in Baltimore in these days, was an M.D., upon whom the muses had, it is said, looked with some favor. His verses, however, were couched in a most erratic vein.

The Bard wrote a great number of fugitive pieces in poetry and prose, which appeared in the local journals of the day.

He was very jealous of Edgar Poe, and endeavored, to the best of his ability, to depreciate him in the estimation of the reading public.

He indulged in alcoholic potations, and, not infrequently, would, under this influence, commit acts which would cause him deep mortification in his sober moments.

One day, while Poe was poring over some books at his publisher's store, the "Bard" entered, shabbily dressed and with unsteady gait.

The poets were unacquainted personally, and did not recognize each other.

The Bard was loquacious and consequential, after the manner of men in his condition.

"How does my volume go off?" asked the Bard of the bookseller.

"Pretty fairly, considering all things," was the reply.

"Considering all things! What do you mean by that?" asked the inebriated rhymester.

"Why, in the first place, the shockingly bad likeness that disfigures the book is complained of," responded the merchant. "The ladies say it is nothing at all like you—not handsome enough. In the second place, the publication does no credit to the printer."

"It is a confounded sight neater work than Poe's," rejoined the Bard. "That fellow, conscious of his ugliness, hadn't the temerity to put his phiz in his book, for fear that it might injure the sale of it. Besides being neater, my volume contains true poetry; whereas Poe's————"

Here the bookseller, perceiving the threatening storm, vainly endeavored to check the garrulous braggart; but the Bard had got upon his pet hobby, and he must needs ride it to the end.

"Who's this Poe, anyhow?" continued he; "an upstart, at best. Here have I been writing for years, and what's my reward? Rags and starvation! Why, sir, there's not a particle of genius in the man; his ideas are wild and discon- nected; his verses hobble, and there's nothing in them that can for a moment excite the sympathy of the reader. Pooh! talk about Poe being a true poet. He may Poe it all his life, and die forgotten."

The Bard wound up breathless at last, by ask- ing the bookseller to advance him some money on the sales of his book, as he had not eaten a morsel of food for two days.

Poe had listened to the abuse of the maudlin M.D., and as he stopped at last, he threw down the book he had been pretending to peruse, and stepping up to his rival, with face glowing with indignation, addressed him:

"You are the Milford Bard, I presume, sir."

"That's me," answered the Bard; "and I ex- pect you are Edgar Poe."

"Exactly so," was the rejoinder. "Now, sir, let me enlighten you on one point on which you appear to be totally ignorant.

"Nature rather missed it when she attempted to instil into your brain even a moiety of true poetry. Write on, and flood the world with your trash,

but don't attempt to pass judgment on the efforts
of others. You are a worse judge than poet.
The Creator didn't intend you should be either."

The Bard cowered beneath the withering
glance of his high-spirited young rival, but, put-
ting on a swaggering air, he retorted, "I'll bet
you five dollars I can write more stanzas in one
hour than you can in a whole day."

Young Poe's lip curled in scorn, although he
seemed half-inclined to pity the wretched inebri-
ate, who, with his hands crammed into his pock-
ets, and an ineffably stupid expression upon his
face, stood swaying from one side to the other.

"I don't think you have five cents to lose,
much less five dollars," he replied ; "but," with a
wink to the bookseller, "I'll accept your challenge."

"Done !" shouted the Bard.

Pencil and paper were furnished, and the
rivals began the tournament of rhymes.

The Bard was strong on his rhyme, although
as much cannot be said for his reason. Poe
wrote poetry. The Bard wrote the veriest non-
sense ; but in *quantity* he tipped the scale. When
the particulars of this unique contest got abroad,

there was many a gibe cracked at the young poet's expense, among the *littérateurs* of Baltimore.

In February, 1829, Poe, learning of the mortal sickness of his adopted mother, Mrs. Allan, hastened to Richmond. He was too late to take a last farewell of her, death having claimed her before the poet had reached his former home.

His visit to the Allan's house seems, however, for the time being, to have reconciled Mr. Allan to Poe, and, through his foster father's influence, a nomination to a scholarship at West Point was obtained.

Poe entered the military academy at West Point on the 1st of July, 1830.

For a time he pursued the exacting course of studies with enthusiasm, headed every class, and seemed delighted with everything.

But soon the unvarying discipline and irksome routine work began to tell upon his sensitive organization, and he chafed under his restraint with ill-concealed impatience.

During this restless period of his sojourn at West Point, he published a third and enlarged edition of his juvenile poems.*

---

* E. Bliss, New York, 1831.

The volume was dedicated to the "United States Corps of Cadets," and although ridiculed by the embryo warriors, was quite generally subscribed for by them at the tolerably high figure of $2.50 for a copy of the book, which was a very thin 12mo of 124 pages, printed on paper of a dirty-brown shade.

General Geo. W. Callum, of the United States army, who was a cadet in the class below Poe at this time, writes of him, "He was a heedless boy, very eccentric, and of course preferred writing verses to solving equations.

"While at the academy, he published a small volume of poems dedicated to Bulwer, in a long random letter. These verses were the source of great merriment with us boys, who considered the author cracked, and the verses ridiculous doggerel.

"Even after the lapse of forty years, I can now recall these lines from ' Isabel :'

> " ' Was not that a fairy ray, Isabel ?
>   How fantastically it fell,
>   With a spiral twist and a swell,
>   And over the wet grass rippled away.
>   Like the tinkling of a bell.' "

His early training, with the petted indulgences of his childhood days, were little calculated to prepare him for the strict *régime* of our severest military school, and he gradually lost his interest in study there, became abstracted, and shirked his military duties as persistently as he had followed them at first.

Finding himself thus totally unadapted, by training and temperament, to the exigencies of the place, he determined to leave it.

At West Point it is necessary, in order to achieve such a step, to obtain permission from the parent or guardian. For this permission, Poe wrote to Mr. Allan, who flatly refused it; this refusal Mr. Poe presented to Col. Thayer, the superintendent of the "Post," who declined interfering with the rules, or to accept the resignation. This was about the period that Poland made the desperate and unfortunate struggle for independence, against the combined powers of Russia, Austria and Prussia, which terminated in the capitulation of Warsaw, and the annihilation of the kingdom. All the cadet's former chivalric vigor had now returned, and with increased vigor. He burned to be a participant in

the affray. But to do this, it was doubly necessary to leave West Point. There was one resource yet left him; this he took. He positively
refused to do duty of any kind, disobeyed all
orders, and, keeping closely to his quarters,
amused himself with caricaturing and pasquin-
ading the professors. There was a gentleman
named Joseph Locke, who had made himself
especially obnoxious, through his pertinacity in
reporting the pranks of the cadets. At West
Point a report is no every-day matter, but a very
serious thing. Each "report" counts a certain
number against the offender, is charged to his
account, and when the whole exceeds a stated
sum, he is liable to dismissal. Poe at this
time, it seems, wrote a lengthy and audacious
lampoon against this Mr. Locke, of which the
following are the only stanzas preserved : —

> "As for Locke, he is all in my eye,
>   May the devil right soon for his soul call.
> He never was known to lie
>   In bed at a *reveille* roll-call.
>
> "John Locke was a notable name :
>   Joe Locke is a greater; in short,
> · The former is well known to fame,
>   But the latter's well known to *report*."

The result of this was just what Poe intended it should be. For some time Colonel Thayer, to whose good offices the young cadet had been personally recommended by General Scott, over-looked these misdemeanors. But at length, the matter becoming too serious, charges were insti-tuted against Poe for "neglect of duty, and disobe-dience of orders" (nothing was said about the lampoons), and he was tried by a court-martial. There were innumerable specifications, to all of which, by way of saving time, he pleaded guilty, although some of them were thoroughly absurd. In a word, he was cashiered *nem. con.*, and went on his way rejoicing.

But not, however, to Poland. The capitula-tion had been effected, and that unfortunate country was no more.

In spite of statements to the contrary, Poe at this time returned to Mr. Allan's house at Rich-mond, and was received by him. Here he met a Miss Royster, to whom he paid attentions, which were favorably received by the lady. But Mr. Allan was determinedly opposed to the match, and a furious quarrel, on this account, occurred between Poe and his foster father.

Poe again left Mr. Allan's house, and took
refuge with his aunt, Mrs. Clemm. Shortly after
the breach between Mr. Allan and Poe, the poet
was amazed by the intelligence that his foster
father had married a beautiful young lady, a
Miss Patterson, of Richmond.

Dr. Griswold, with a semblance of shame that
is unaccountable as emanating from him, relates,
in a learned *foot-note* in his memoir, full of
dark suggestions, quoted liberally from Sir
Thomas Browne, that there is another side to the
story of the final quarrel between Mr. Allan and
Poe, in which Miss Patterson is supposed to
figure. We regard this innuendo as perhaps the
most diabolical of the many unjustifiable be-
smirchings which Griswold has heaped upon
Poe; for, whatever may have been the poet's
faults, that he was chaste as ice, all *competent*
authorities unite in attesting. *Honi soit qui mal y
pense.* He was romantic, chivalrous, not sensual.

But Griswold was a sensualist and a libertine
of a very low order. He knew no standard of
morality higher than his own.

With the birth of a son to Mr. Allan by his
second wife, Poe's hopes of inheriting received a

final blow, and in the congenial society of his aunt and his fairy cousin Virginia, to whom he was destined to be a Paul, he devoted himself to literary work, not at the outset, it would seem, for profit, but as a diversion for his otherwise idle hours.

Until very recently, the whereabouts of Poe during this period have been veiled from his biographers, and the gap left unfilled until now, except by the mendacities of Dr. Griswold. The doctor, not having any facts at hand to mortise into this gap, comes to the rescue of his impotent researches, and, after his usual manner, placidly *invents* another piece of defamatory fiction.

"His contributions," says Dr. Griswold, "attracted little attention, and his hopes of gaining a living in this way being disappointed, he enlisted in the army as a private soldier. How long he remained in the army I have not been able to ascertain. He was recognized by officers who had known him at West Point, and efforts were made privately, but with prospects, to obtain for him a commission, when it was discovered by his friends that he had deserted." The facts are, on the written testimony of Mrs.

Clemm, that at this time his friends were seeking
for him a commission, and it is folly to believe,
when the prospects were favorable for his securing a higher position, that he would have enlisted
as a private, and thus deliberately and unneces-
sarily have incurred the penalty and disgrace of
desertion. That Mrs. Clemm, at least, was in
full knowledge of his whereabouts at this time,
is evident from her statement made in this regard,
that Poe never slept one night away from home
until after he was married. It is futile to say, as
one of Poe's friendly contemporaries has said,
that such an audacious rumor should never have
obtained admission into a memoir of Poe, and
that it never would have done so, had proper
inquiries been made. Griswold never cared to
make inquiries; and if he had, he was not the
man ever to have made *proper* inquiries.

An important event in the poet's life was
his appearance as a competitor for the prizes
offered by the proprietor of the "Saturday
Visitor," at Baltimore. The prizes were, one
for the best tale and one for the best poem.
Dr. Griswold states that, attracted by the beauty of Poe's penmanship, the committee, with-

out opening any of the other manuscripts, voted
unanimously that the prizes should be paid to
"the first of geniuses who had written legibly."
On the contrary, there appeared in the "Visitor,"
after the awards were made, complimentary
comments over the committee's own signatures.
They said, among other things, that *all* the tales
offered by Poe were far *better than the best*
offered by others; adding "that they thought it a
duty to call public attention to them in these columns in that marked manner, since they possessed
a singular force and beauty, and were eminently
distinguished by a rare, vigorous and poetical
imagination, a rich style, a fertile invention and
varied and curious learning."

The committee comprised three of the most
prominent citizens of Baltimore at that time,
Messrs. John P. Kennedy, James H. Miller and
J. H. B. Latrobe.

The story of this award and its sequence has
been graphically related by Mr. Latrobe, who
is now a hale old gentleman of seventy-six
years.

We had the pleasure of hearing the following
narrative from Mr. Latrobe's own lips : —

"About the year 1832, there was a newspaper in Baltimore, called 'Saturday Review'— an ephemeral publication, that aimed at amusing its readers with light literary productions rather than the news of the day. One of its efforts was to produce original tales; and to this end it offered on this occasion two prizes, one for the best story and the other for the best short poem — one hundred dollars for the first, and fifty dollars for the last. The judges appointed by the editor of the 'Visitor' were the late John P. Kennedy, Dr. James H. Miller (now deceased) and myself, and accordingly we met, one pleasant afternoon, in the back parlor of my house on Mulberry Street, and, seated round a table garnished with some old wine and some good cigars, commenced our critical labors. As I happened then to be the youngest of the three, I was required to open the packages of prose and poetry, respectively, and read the contents. Alongside of me was a basket to hold what we might reject.

"I remember well that the first production taken from the top of the prose pile was in a woman's hand, written very distinctly, as, indeed, were all the articles submitted, and so neatly that it

seemed a pity not to award to it a prize. It was
ruthlessly criticized, however, for it was ridicu-
lously bad — namby-pamby in the extreme — full
of sentiment, and of the school then known as
the Laura Matilda school. The first page would
have consigned it to the basket as our critical
guillotine beheaded it. Gallantry, however,
caused it to be read through, when in it went,
along with the envelope containing the name of
the writer, which, of course, remained unknown.
The next piece I have no recollection of, except
that a dozen lines consigned it to the basket. I
remember that the third, perhaps the fourth, production was recognized as a translation from the
French, with a terrific *dénoûement*. It was a
poor translation, too; for, falling into literal accuracy, the writer had, in many places, followed
the French idioms. The story was not without
merit, but the Sir Fretful Plagiary of a translator
described the charge of Sheridan in the 'Critic,'
of being like a beggar who had stolen another
man's child and clothed it in his own rags. Of
the remaining productions I have no recollection.
Some were condemned after a few sentences had
been read. Some were laid aside for reconsid-

eration — not many. These last failed to pass muster afterwards, and the committee had about made up their minds that there was nothing before them to which they would award a prize, when I noticed a small quarto-bound book that had until then accidentally escaped attention, possibly because so unlike, externally, the bundles of manuscript that it had to compete with. Opening it, an envelope with a motto corresponding with one in the book appeared, and we found that our prose examination was still incomplete. Instead of the common cursive manuscript, the writing was in Roman characters — an imitation of printing. I remember that while reading the first page to myself, Mr. Kennedy and the doctor had filled their glasses and lit their cigars, and when I said that we seemed at last to have a prospect of awarding the prize, they laughed as though they doubted it, and settled themselves in their comfortable chairs as I began to read. I had not proceeded far, before my colleagues became as much interested as myself. The first tale finished, I went to the second, then to the next, and did not stop until I had gone through the volume, interrupted only by such exclamations as 'Capital!' 'Excellent!' 'How odd!' and the like from my companions. There was genius in everything they listened to; there was no uncertain grammar, no feeble phraseology, no ill-placed punctuation, no worn-out truisms, no strong thought elaborated into weakness. Logic and imagination were combined in rare consistency. Sometimes the writer created in his mind a world of his own, and then described it — a world so weird, so strange —

> 'Far down by the dim lake of Auber;
> In the misty mid-region of Wier;
> Far down by the dank tarn of Auber,
> In the ghoul-haunted woodland of Wier'—

and withal so fascinating, so wonderfully graphic, that it seemed for the moment to have all the truth of a reality. There was an analysis of complicated facts — an unravelling of circumstantial evidence that won the lawyer judges — an amount of accurate scientific knowledge that charmed their accomplished colleague — a pure classic diction that delighted all three.

"When the reading was completed, there was a difficulty of choice. Portions of the tales were read again, and finally the committee selected

'A MS. found in a Bottle.' One of the series was called 'A Descent into the Maelstrom,' and this was at one time preferred. I cannot now recall the names of all the tales. There must have been six or eight. But all the circumstances of the selection ultimately made, have been so often since referred to in conversation, that my memory has been kept fresh, and I see my fellow-judges over their wine and cigars, in their easy-chairs — both genial, hearty men, in pleasant mood, as distinctly now as though I were describing an event of yesterday.

"Having made the selection and awarded the one hundred dollar prize, not, as has been said most unjustly and ill-naturedly, because the manuscript was legible, but because of the unquestionable genius and great originality of the writer, we were at liberty to open the envelope that identified him, and there we found in the note, whose motto corresponded with that of the little volume, the name, which I see you anticipate, of Edgar Allan Poe.

"The statement of Dr. Griswold's life, prefixed to the common edition of Poe's works, that 'it was unanimously decided by the committee that

the prize should be given to the first genius who
had written legibly — not another MS. was un·
folded,' is absolutely untrue.

"Refreshed by this most unexpected change
in the character of the contributions, the committee refilled their glasses and relit their cigars,
and the reader began upon the poetry. This,
although better in the main than the prose, was
bad enough, and when we had gone more or
less thoroughly over the pile of manuscript, two
pieces only were deemed worthy of consideration. The title of one was 'The Colisseum,' the
written printing of which told that it was Poe's.
The title of the other I have forgotten; but upon
opening the accompanying envelope we found
that the author was Mr. John H. Hewitt, still
living in Baltimore, and well known, I believe,
in the musical world, both as a poet and composer. I am not prepared to say that the committee may not have been biased in awarding
the fifty dollar prize to Mr. Hewitt by the fact
that they had already given the one hundred
dollar prize to Mr. Poe. I recollect, however,
that we agreed that, under the circumstances,
the excellence of Mr. Hewitt's poem deserved a

reward, and we gave the smaller prize to him with clear consciences.

"I believe that up to this time not one of the committee had ever seen Mr. Poe, and it is my impression that I was the only one that had ever heard of him. When his name was read, I remembered that on one occasion Mr. Wm. Gwynn, a prominent member of the bar of Baltimore, had shown me the very neat manuscript of a poem called 'Al Aaraaf,' which he spoke of as indicative of a tendency to anything but the business of matter-of-fact life. Those of my hearers who are familiar with the poet's works will recollect it as one of his earlier productions. Although Mr. Gwynn, being an admirable lawyer, was noted as the author of wise and witty epigrams in verse, 'Al Aaraaf' was not in his vein, and what he said of the writer had not prepared me for the productions before the committee. His name, I am sure, was not at the time a familiar one.

"The next number of the 'Saturday Visitor' contained the 'MS. found in a Bottle,' and announced the author. My office, in those days, was in the building still occupied by the Mechan-

ics' Bank, and I was seated at my desk, on the
Monday following the publication of the tale,
when a gentleman entered and introduced himself as the writer, saying that he came to thank
me, as one of the committee, for the award in his
favor.   Of this interview, the only one I ever had
with Mr. Poe, my recollection is very distinct
indeed, and it requires but a small effort of imagination to place him before me now as plainly
almost as I see any one of my audience.   He
was, if anything, below the middle size, and yet
could not be described as a small man.   His figure was remarkably good, and he carried himself
erect and well, as one who had been trained to
it.   He was dressed in black, and his frock coat
was buttoned to his throat, where it met the
black stock, then almost universally worn.   Not
a particle of white was visible.   Coat, hat, boots
and gloves had very evidently seen their best
days, but so far as mending and brushing go,
everything had been done, apparently, to make
them presentable.   On most men his clothes
would have looked shabby and seedy; but there
was something about this man that prevented one
from criticizing his garments, and the details I

have mentioned were only recalled afterwards. The impression made, however, was that the award made in Mr. Poe's favor was not inopportune. *Gentleman* was written all over him. His manner was easy and quiet, and although he came to return thanks for what he regarded as deserving them, there was nothing obsequious in what he said or did. His features I am unable to describe in detail. His forehead was high, and remarkable for the great development of the temple. This was the characteristic of his head which you noticed at once, and which I have never forgotten. The expression of his face was grave, almost sad, except when he was engaged in conversation, when it became animated and changeable. His voice, I remember, was very pleasing in its tone, and well modulated, almost rhythmical, and his words were well chosen and unhesitating. Taking a seat, we conversed a while on ordinary topics, and he informed me that Mr. Kennedy, my colleague in the commitee, on whom he had already called, had either given or promised to give him a letter to the 'Southern Literary Messenger,' which he hoped would procure him employment. I asked him whether he was then occupied with any literary labor. He replied that he was engaged on a voyage to the moon; and at once went into a somewhat learned disquisition upon the laws of gravity, the height of the earth's atmosphere, and the capacities of balloons, warming in his speech as he proceeded. Presently, speaking in the first person, he began the voyage. After describing the preliminary arrangements, as you will find them set forth in one of his tales called 'Adventures of one Hans Pfaal,' and leaving the earth, and becoming more and more animated, he described his sensations as he ascended higher and higher, until at last he reached the point in space where the moon's attraction overcame that of the earth, when there was a sudden *bouleversement* of the car, and a great confusion among its tenants. By this time the speaker had become so excited, spoke so rapidly, gesticulating much, that when the turn-upside-down took place, and he clapped his hands and stamped with his foot, by way of emphasis, I was carried along with him, and, for aught to the contrary that I now remember, may have fancied myself the companion of his aerial journey. The climax of the tale was the reversal

I have mentioned. When he had finished his description, he apologized for his excitability, which he laughed at himself. The conversation then turned upon other subjects, and soon afterward he took his leave. I never saw him more. Dr. Griswold's statement that 'Mr. Kennedy accompanied him (Poe) to a clothing store and purchased for him a respectable suit, with a change of linen, and sent him to a bath,' is a sheer fabrication."

In the Mr. Kennedy of this jovial committee, Poe found a friend, who continued one of the poet's staunchest supporters to the day of his death.

At this time he attended to Poe's material needs, gave him free access to his home and its comforts, the use of a horse for exercise when required, and lifted him out of the depths into which his depression and disappointments had sunk him. Mr. Hewitt relates that Poe visited the office of the "Minerva," after the announcement of the prizes, and besought him to waive his claim to the prize, but to receive the money, which Poe was willing he should have. He only wanted the honors, which, he had been informed, he had fairly earned, for his poetry as well as for his prose. Mr. Hewitt did not, of course, defer to this pardonable but extraordinary request, and Poe's first laurel wreath was robbed of a bright leaf.

In 1834, Mr. Allan died, leaving an infant child, who supplanted Poe in his expected heir-ship.

Not a penny was left to the heir expectant, who had been permitted to grow to manhood, fed with the delusive hopes that, at the most critical period of his life, turned to dust and ashes, and left him to the mercies of an uncharitable and unsympathizing world.

CHAPTER IV.

1834 — 1838.

First Contributions to Periodicals — Engagement with the
"Southern Literary Messenger" — Griswold's Pettiness —
Critical Reviews — J. K. Paulding's Encomiums — Mar-
riage with his cousin, Virginia Clemm — Melancholy in
Solitude — Susceptibility to Drink — Innocence of Motive —
Withdrawal from the "Messenger" — Engagement on the
"New York Quarterly Review" — Mr. William Gowans'
Reviews — A Notable Review — First Prose Book, "Ar-
thur Gordon Pym " — Its success in England.

WHILE in Baltimore at this time, Poe
wrote and published several reviews and
stories, among which was the "Hans
Pfaal," mentioned by Mr. Latrobe, which Gris·
wold leaves us to infer is an imitation of Locke's
celebrated moon hoax; whereas Poe's story ap
peared *three weeks* before Locke's story saw the
light.

During this year (1834), Mr. Thomas W.
White, of Richmond, launched a new literary
enterprise, "The Southern Literary Messenger."

Mr. Kennedy was among the number invited to contribute to the pages of the new magazine.

Mr. Kennedy's time did not, however, admit of his acceptance of Mr. White's offer; but he did not lose the opportunity to recommend his protégé to apply as his substitute.

That Poe was successful in his application to Mr. White, is well known.

The poet sent several specimens of his literary work, and in March, 1835, one of them, " Berenice," was published.

Mr. White was so well pleased with Poe's contributions, that he made Poe an offer to come to Richmond, to undertake a department on the magazine.

In response to this proposition the poet wrote :

" You ask me if I would be willing to come on to Richmond if you should have occasion for my services during the coming winter. I reply that nothing would give me greater pleasure. I have been desirous for some time past of paying a visit to Richmond, and would be glad of any reasonable excuse for so doing. Indeed, I am anxious to settle myself in that city, and if, by any chance, you hear of a situation likely to suit me, I would gladly accept it, were the salary even the merest trifle. I should, indeed, feel myself greatly indebted to you if, through your means, I could accomplish this object. What you say in the conclusion of your letter, in relation to the supervision of proof-sheets, gives me reason to hope that possibly you might find something for me to do in your office. If so, I should be very glad, for at present only a very small portion of my time is employed."

Mr. Kennedy, in response to a letter of inquiry from Mr. White, had previously written, —

"Dear Sir, — Poe did right in referring to me. He is very clever with his pen — classical and scholarlike. He wants experience and direction, but I have no doubt he can be made very useful to you; and, poor fellow! he is *very* poor. I told him to write something for every number of your magazine, and that you might find it to your advantage to give him some permanent employ. He has a volume of very *bizarre* tales in the hands of —— in Philadelphia, who for a year past has been promising to publish them. This young fellow is highly imaginative, and a little given to the *terrific.* He is at work upon a tragedy, but I have turned him to drudging upon whatever may make money, and I have no doubt you and he will find your account in each other."

An amusing instance of Griswold's pettiness, and want of common-sense judgment even, in his endeavor to demean the position and character of his subject as much as possible, is found in the following paragraph in the biography. Speaking of the poet's connection with the "Literary Messenger," he writes, "In the next number of the 'Messenger,' Mr. White announced

that Poe was its editor, or, in other words, that
he had made arrangements with a gentleman of
approved literary taste and attainments, to whose
especial management the editorial department
would be confided, and it was declared that this
gentleman would 'devote his exclusive attention to
his work.'" Having put this down in black and
white, following his statement that Mr. White
was a man of much purity of character, the re-
doubtable biographer evidently feels that he has
set Poe up a peg too high, and immediately
planes him down to an endurable level in the
next sentence: "Poe continued, however, to reside in Baltimore, and it is probable that he was
engaged only as a *general contributor* and *writer
of critical notices of books*." Apropos of these
book reviews, Dr. Griswold dismisses them as
follows: "He continued in Baltimore till September. In this period he wrote several long
reviews, which for the most part were abstracts
of works, rather than critical discussions." As a
matter of fact, the "Messenger" was in its seventh
month, with about four hundred subscribers, when
Poe assumed the editorship. Poe remained with
this journal until the end of its second year, by

which time its circulation had been increased fourfold. A contemporary of Poe writes that "the success of the 'Messenger' has been justly attributable to Poe's exertions on its behalf, but especially to the skill, honesty and audacity of the criticism under the editorial head. The review of 'Norman Leslie' may be said to have introduced a new era in our critical literature."

This review was followed up continuously by others of equal force and character. Of the review of Drake and Halleck, Mr. J. K. Paulding says, in a private letter, "I think it one of the finest specimens of criticism ever published in this country."

But Griswold could see nothing in Poe's book reviews of which he cared to speak, for reasons which will be apparent later.

On the eve of setting out for Richmond, the poet, who felt that his prospects in life had now become permanently settled, married his cousin, Virginia Clemm, in whom he had manifested a tender interest since his first meeting with her.

He had interested himself in educating her when she was but ten years of age, and now at fourteen, she was intellectually, maturely developed.

Poe's relatives, both on his side and that of the wife, opposed this match, for the lady was very delicate and already marked as a victim to consumption, which prevailed in the family. But this modern Paul and his Virginia were not to be separated without taking upon themselves firmer ties than those of mere friendship, and they were duly married in Baltimore, although they did not live together until a year later, when, in deference to the wishes of the family, they were remarried in Richmond, by the late Rev. John Johns, Bishop of Virginia.

In his solitary moments, while separated from his beloved child-wife, Poe seems to have been deeply afflicted with the despairing melancholy which, in his later years, wrought upon him the direst effects. At this time he wrote to his friend, Mr. Kennedy, as follows : —

RICHMOND, September 11, 1835.

Dear Sir, — I received a letter from Dr. Miller, in which he tells me you are in town.

I hasten, therefore, to write you and express by letter what I have always found it impossible to express orally, — my deep sense of gratitude for your frequent and ineffectual assistance and kindness.

Through your influence, Mr. White has been induced to employ me in assisting him in with the editorial duties of his magazine, at a salary of five hundred and twenty dollars per annum.

The situation is agreeable to me for many reasons, but, alas! it appears to me that nothing can give me pleasure or the slightest gratification.

Excuse me, my dear sir, if in this letter you find much incoherency; my feelings, at this moment, are pitiable indeed.

I am suffering under a depression of spirits such as I have never felt before. I have struggled in vain against the influence of this melancholy; *you will believe me* when I say that I am still miserable, in spite of the great improvement in my circumstances. I say you will believe me, and for this simple reason, that a man who is writing for *effect*, does not write thus. My heart is open before you; if it be worth reading, read it. I am wretched, and know not why. Console me! for you can. But let it be quickly, or it will be too late. Write me immediately; convince me that it is worth one's while—that it is at all necessary—to live, and you will prove yourself indeed my friend. Persuade me to do what is right. I do mean this. I do not mean that you should consider what I now write you a jest. Oh, pity me! for I feel that my words are incoherent; but I will recover myself. You will not fail to see that I am suffering under a depression of spirits which will ruin me should it be long continued. Write me, then, and quickly; urge me to do what is right. Your words will have more weight with me than the words of others, for you were my friend when no one else was. Fail not, as you value your peace of mind hereafter.   E. A. Poe.

How little the peculiar temperament of Poe
was understood by those with whom he was
associated, and how little of that precious sympathy for which his sensitive soul pined was vouch-
safed him, is evident from the following matter-
of-fact, but kindly intended, letter from his best
friend, in answer to his despairing plaint : —

"I am sorry to see you in such plight as your letter shows
you in. It is strange that just at this time, when everybody
is praising you, and when fortune is beginning to smile upon
your hitherto wretched circumstances, you should be invaded
by these blue-devils. It belongs, however, to your age and
temper to be thus buffeted — but be assured, it only wants a
little resolution to master the adversary forever. You will
doubtless do well henceforth in literature, and add to your
comforts as well as to your reputation, which, it gives me
great pleasure to assure you, is everywhere rising in popular
esteem."

During this period of isolation, Poe's susceptibility to the influence of drink became manifest.

The subject of Poe's alleged intemperance is
one that has given rise to an amount of righteous
condemnation that would have overwhelmed and
obliterated the reputation of an ordinary writer.

Mr. N. P. Willis writes, "We heard from one
who knew him well (what should be stated in all

mention of his lamentable irregularities), that with a single glase of wine his whole nature was reversed; the demon became uppermost, and, although none of the usual signs of intoxication were visible, his *will* was palpably insane."

On this point Mr. Thomas C. Latto writes, "Whatever his lapses might have been, whatever he might say of himself (Burns was equally incautious, and equally garrulous in his aberrations), the American poet was never a sot; yet the charge has been made against him again and again."

One of the most respected clergymen in Massachusetts, who knew Poe well during the later years of the poet's life, most emphatically assured me, in a recent conversation, that Poe was not a drunkard. "Why (he said), I, the most innocent of divinity students at the time (1847), while walking with Poe, and feeling thirsty, pressed him to take a glass of wine with me. He declined, but finally compromised by taking a glass of ale with me. Almost instantly a great change came over him. Previously engaged in an indescribably eloquent conversation, he became as if paralyzed, and with compressed lips and fixed, glaring eyes, returned, without uttering a word, to the house which we were visiting. For hours, the strange spell hung over him. He seemed a changed being, as if stricken by some peculiar phase of insanity."

We mention this as an act of simple justice to the poet, and to make apparent the falsity of the accounts of Poe's orgies and protracted indulgences, as recorded by Griswold and others of the poet's villifiers.

He never drank, never could have drunk, to excess. His fault then was not in his *excessive* indulgence in intoxicating drinks, but in his exceptional susceptibility to the influence of liquor.

There is no evidence that his weakness was in the insatiable *craving* for stimulants, common to drunkards. When he drank, at times, it was more frequently with the innocent intent, common to the large majority of mankind who are able to take a single glass with impunity, of exchanging a social pledge with a friend or companion. Nature had made him an unfortunate exception; and will it not be generally admitted that any inherited or constitutional weakness is less amenable to reason, than one which is merely the result of an artificial or acquired taste?

Poe, it would seem, never resorted to liquor, even for the pardonable necessity of stimulating his literary inspirations. Such a sequence was impossible to his indulgence in what is to many a fortunate and desirable support.

When engaged in writing, his sensitive organization rendered any stimulant stronger than coffee fatal to his work, and even that pleasant and comparatively innocent beverage could be taken but sparingly by him. One of the causes of his isolation from society in the later years of his life, was his sensitiveness to his exceptional weakness, which placed him in an awkward position, from his native courtesy, when obliged, for self-protection, to decline even touching a *single* glass of wine.

Referring to Poe's retirement from the "Messenger," which took place in 1837, Griswold writes, "Poe's irregularities frequently interrupted the kindness, and finally exhausted the patience, of his generous though methodical employer, and in the number of the "Messenger" for January 1837, he thus took leave of its readers : —

"*Mr. Poe's* attention being called in another direction, he will decline, with the present num-

ber, the editorial duties of the 'Messenger.' His
Critical Notices for this month end with Professor
Anthon's "Cicero"— what follows is from another
hand. With the best wishes to the magazine,
and to its few foes, as well as many friends, he is
now desirous of bidding all parties a peaceful
farewell."

So far from dismissing the poet on account of
drunkenness, Mr. White parted from him with
reluctance ; and Griswold's contemptible meanness is again exhibited in the suppression, in his
memoir, of Mr. White's letter to his subscribers,
which appeared in the *identical number* of the
"Messenger" which contained Poe's note of resignation.

In this note, the proprietor paid a handsome
compliment to the marked ability of his editor,
acknowledged the success of the magazine under
his direction, and added, "Mr. Poe, however,
will continue to furnish its columns, from time to
time, with the effusions of his vigorous and popular pen."

Griswold knew well that Poe resigned, owing
to a flattering invitation which he received from
Professors Anthon, Henry and Hawks to come

to New York and join them in their new literary enterprise, "The New York Quarterly Review."

In the letter of Dr. Hawks is sounded the key-note to which Poe responded in his after-work with an implacable devotion that struck terror to the hearts of all those who crossed the path of his merciless pen. Dr. Hawks writes, "I wish you to fall in with your *broad-axe* [the italics are the doctor's] amidst this miserable literary trash that surrounds us. I believe you have the will, and I know you will have the ability."

In acceptance of Dr. Hawks' invitation, Poe removed to New York, and took up his residence at No. 113 Carmine Street in that city.

A valuable contribution to the ana of Poe has been left by Mr. William Gowans, the Scotch bibliopolist, of New York, widely known and respected by the book-selling and book-reading community. Mr. Gowans, as it happened, resided in the same house with Poe at this time, and writing of the criticisms of Poe by his contemporaries, as well as his domestic *ménage* which he had a rare opportunity of observing, he says, —

"The characters drawn of Poe by his various

biographers and critics may, with safety, be pronounced an excess of exaggeration; but this is
not to be much wondered at, when it is taken
into consideration that these men were rivals,
either as poets or prose writers, and it is well
known that such are generally as jealous of each
other as are the ladies who are handsome, or
those who desire to be considered possessed of
the coveted quality. It is an old truism, and as
true as it old, 'that in the midst of counsels there
is safety.' I, therefore, will also show you my
opinion of this gifted but unfortunate man. It
may be estimated as worth little, but it has this
merit: it comes from an eye and ear witness,
and this, it must be remembered, is the very
highest of legal evidence.

"For eight months or more, one house contained us, one table fed us. During that time I
saw much of him, and had an opportunity of
conversing with him often, and I must say, I
never saw him in the least affected by liquor,·
nor knew him to descend to any kind of vice;
while he was one of the most courteous, gentlemanly and intelligent companions I have ever
met during my journeyings and haltings through

divers divisions of the globe.   Besides, he had an extra inducement to be a good man, as well as a good husband, for he had a wife of matchless beauty and loveliness.

"Her eyes could match those of any houri, and her face defy the genius of Canova to imitate; a temper and disposition of surpassing sweetness. She seemed, withal, as much devoted to him and his every interest as a young mother is to her first-born."

Among other critical articles written by Poe for the "Review" at this time, was a lengthy criticism on Stephens' "Incidents of Travels in Egypt, Arabia, Petrea and the Holy Land."   The poet made an elaborate showing-up of the traveller's misconceptions of the biblical prophecies, as well as of some important mistranslations in Ezekiel and Isaiah.

This article created a sensation, although it aroused the antagonism of such men as Griswold, and others of his ilk, some of whom yet live to void their venom upon the fair fame of the fearless adversary, with whom in life they dared not to measure swords.

During his residence in New York, at this

time, Poe published, in book form, a story which he had begun several months before in the "Literary Messenger,"—"Arthur Gordon Pym." The work was issued by Harper & Brothers. The title-page reads as follows:—

"The Narrative of Arthur Gordon Pym, of Nantucket: comprising the Details of a Mutiny and Atrocious Butchery on board the American Brig 'Grampus,' on her way to the South Seas; with an Account of the Recapture of the Vessel by the Survivors; their Shipwreck, and subsequent Horrible Sufferings from Famine; their Deliverance by means of the British Schooner Jane Gray; the brief Cruise of this latter Vessel in the Antarctic Ocean; her Capture, and the Massacre of the Crew among a Group of Islands in the 84th parallel of southern latitude; together with the incredible Adventures and Discoveries still further South, to which that distressing calamity gave rise."

The work was not appreciated by the American public, and less than a thousand copies were disposed of by the publishers. In England, however, it was highly successful, running through several editions within a short time.

Griswold says, "that the publishers sent one hundred copies to England, and being mistaken, at first, for a narrative of real experiences, it was advertised to be reprinted; but a discovery of its character, I believe, prevented such a result." It will be noted that the facts again tip the scale, against the balance of Griswold's fiction, in this instance.

CHAPTER V.

OE remained in New York but a year.
The metropolis was not then the Mecca
of magazinists and critics that it has
come to be now, and Philadelphia seemed then
to offer superior advantages to the poet-critic for
regular employment.

(88)

Near the end of the year 1838, Poe removed to Philadelphia. There Wm. E. Burton, the famous comedian, had established the "Gentleman's Magazine." The poet joined its corps of contributors, and in less than six months his brilliant experience with the "Messenger" was repeated, and the editor's chair was assigned to him. In this position he worked two hours a day, at a salary of ten dollars per week. This engagement gave him ample time for other literary duties, and he wrote for other journals, among which was the "Literary Examiner," of Pittsburgh, Pa. Some of his best prose tales were done at this time, when the yoke of privation sat but lightly upon his shoulders.

"Ligeia," his favorite tale, written at this time, was inspired by a dream, although none but his charmed circle of intimates were permitted to know of the inner life which gave it birth. To these he often spoke, writes Mrs. Whitman, "of the imageries and incidents of his inner life, as more vivid and veritable than those of his outer experience."

On a manuscript copy of one of his later poems, he refers, in a pencilled note, to the vision that inspired "Ligeia :"

"All that I have here expressed was actually present to me. Remember the mental condition which gave rise to 'Ligeia,'—recall the passage of which I spoke, and observe the coincidence."

"I regard these visions," he says, "even as they arise, with an awe which, in some measure, moderates or tranquillizes the ecstasy. I so regard them through a conviction that this ecstasy, in itself, is of a character supernal to nature,— is a glimpse of the spirit's inner world." "He had," writes Mrs. Whitman, "that constitutional determination to reverie which, according to De Quincey, alone enables man to dream magnificently, and which, as we have said, made his dreams realities, and his life a dream.

"His mind was, indeed, a Haunted Palace, echoing to the footfalls of angels and demons."

"No man," said Poe, "has recorded, no man has dared to record, the wonders of his inner life."

"The Fall of the House of Usher" also appeared at this time. Even Griswold was moved to accord to these tales "the unquestionable stamp of genius."

He writes of them, "The analyses of the growth of madness in one, and the thrilling revelations of the existence of a first wife in the person of a second, in the other, are made with consummate skill ; and the strange and solemn and fascinating beauty which informs the style and invests the circumstances of both, drugs the mind, and makes us forget the improbabilities of their general design."

"The Fall of the House of Usher" incorporated the poem of "The Haunted Palace," which Griswold ventured to mention as a specimen of Poe's so-called plagiarisms "scarcely paralleled for their audacity in all literary history."

Poe has been accused of taking "The Haunted Palace" from Longfellow's " Beleaguered City." The "doctor" states that Longfellow's poem appeared a *few weeks* after "The Haunted Palace ;" but that it had been written long before, and had been in Poe's possession for a time. The fact is, that Poe's poem had appeared long before Longfellow's, and in two different publications.

The same imperturbable authority which presumes placidly to state that Poe was not remarkably original in invention, owing to these sundry plagiarisms, classes his story of " The Pit and the Pendulum" under the same head. This, he says, was borrowed from a story, entitled " *Vivenzio*," or "Italian Vengeance," by the author of " The First and Last Dinner," in "Blackwood's Magazine." These stories have been carefully compared (*not* by Dr. Griswold), and their *only* similarity is in the fact that both stories are founded upon the idea of a collapsing room, for which authenticated historical record, and not the creative power of the writers, is to be credited. In plot or construction, there is not the slightest resemblance between these stories.

The most flagrant plagiarism alleged against Poe by Dr. Griswold was that of the publishing of the " Manual of Conchology," which, it is charged, was a copy, nearly verbatim, of " The Text-book of Conchology," by Captain Thomas Brown, printed in Glasgow in 1833. He writes, " Mr. Poe actually took out a copyright for the American edition of Captain Brown's work, and, omitting all mention of the English original, pretended, in the preface, to have been under great obligations to several scientific gentlemen of this city."

Although this story could have, at the time of the original publication of Griswold's memoir, been easily disproved, no one of Poe's friends took the trouble to investigate this charge; and his rivals and enemies were only well pleased to accept the statement of Griswold as truthful. Most of them had been pretty roughly handled — pilloried by the poet's merciless pen; and although they may have deserved his strictures, which, however severe, never stooped to deliberate falsification, they were, nevertheless, goaded to the bitterest enmity by his scathing *exposé* of their shortcomings.

Therefore, it is to be presumed, this story of the wholesale appropriation of the English author's book was as a toothsome morsel in their cup of bitterness.

But some ten years after this falsehood had gone on record, it was most authoritatively disproved in the columns of the "Home Journal," New York, by Professor Wyatt, a Scotch scientist, who, it is understood, was not in the country at the time the charge against Poe was orignally published.

This gentleman had, it seems, become ac-

quainted with Poe while the poet was connected
with the "Gentleman's Magazine," at the period
of which we are now writing, and had engaged
him to assist in the compilation of several works
on natural history.

A comparison of Brown's "Text-book" with
Poe and Wyatt's "Manual" evidences that they
bear some resemblance, both being founded on
the system of Lamarck; but it would be as absurd
to charge that the American book is plagiarized
from the English, as it would be to term "Hook-
er's School Physiology" a plagiarism from Olm-
sted's, because both treat of certain subjects in
common.

As musical composers frequently vie with each
other in setting their scores to the same subject,
so authors may be permitted to evolve from a
given subject, even if previously appropriated,
the new creations moulded by the emanations of
their own peculiar creative powers; and, by
matter-of-fact minds, incapable of sensing delicate distinctions, poets from Shakspeare down to
Aldrich have been, and will continue to be, ad-
judged guilty of arrant plagiarisms.

In the autumn of 1839, Poe published his first

collection of tales in two volumes under the
title, "Tales of the Arabesque and Grotesque."
This issue included "Ligeia," and "The Fall of
the House of Usher," with others of his notable
imaginative compositions. These stories were,
at the time, caviare to the general reading public
to which they were addressed; but they won
favor with the very limited circle of literary people, whose favor was worth the while, although
the poet probably reaped no significant pecuniary
reward from their publication.

Dr. Griswold's account of Poe's alleged secession from the "Gentleman's Magazine," which he
states occurred in 1840, wilfully misrepresents the
facts, after the manner of this vindictive villifier.

After mentioning a personal correspondence
between Burton and Poe, in which the views of
the latter, whatever they may have been, are
carefully suppressed, Dr. Griswold romances
as follows: "He [Burton] was absent nearly
a fortnight, and on returning he found that his
printers had not received a line of copy, but that
Poe had prepared the prospectus of a new
monthly, and obtained transcripts of his subscription and account books, to be used in a scheme

for supplanting him.   He encountered his associate late in the evening, at one of his accustomed haunts, and said, 'Mr. Poe, I am astonished. Give me my manuscripts, so that I can attend to the duties which you have so shamefully neglected, and when you are sober we will settle.' Poe interrupted him with, 'Who are you that presume to address me in this manner? Burton, I am the editor of the "Penn Magazine," and you are — hiccup — a *fool!'* Of course, this ended his relations with the 'Gentleman's.'" That this alleged conversation, so plausibly narrated as to pass current, *nem. con.*, were it not for the existence of more reliable documentary evidence, is an audacious invention, will be apparent from the written testimony given of a gentleman connected with the "Gentleman's Magazine" at this time as publisher, Charles W. Alexander, Esq., the founder of the "Philadelphia Saturday Evening Post."

In a letter to T. W. Clarke, Esq., proprietor of the "Museum," published at that time in Philadelphia, Mr. Alexander writes as follows : —

PHILADELPHIA, Oct. 20th, 1850.

My dear Sir, — I very cheerfully reply to your request made in reference to our friend Edgar Allan Poe.

I well remember his connection with the "Gentleman's Magazine," of which Mr. Burton was editor, and myself the publisher, at the period referred to in connection with Mr. Poe.

The absence of the principal editor on professional duties left the matter frequently in the hands of Mr. Poe, whose unfortunate failing may have occasioned some disappointment in the preparation of a particular article expected from *him*, but never interfering with the regular publication of the "Gentleman's Magazine," as its monthly issue was never interrupted upon any occasion, either from Mr. Poe's deficiency, or from any other cause, during my publication of it, embracing the whole time of Mr. Poe's connection with it. That Mr. Poe had faults seriously detrimental to his own interests, none, of course, will deny. They were, unfortunately, too well known in the literary circles of Philadelphia, were there any disposition to conceal them. But he alone was the sufferer, and not those who received the benefit of his pre-eminent talents, however irregular his habits or uncertain his contributions may occasionally have been.

I had long and familiar intercourse with him, and very cheerfully embrace the opportunity which you now offer of bearing testimony to the uniform *gentleness of disposition* and kindness of heart which distinguished Mr. Poe in all my intercourse with him. With all his faults, he was a gentleman; which is more than can be said of some who have undertaken the ungracious task of blacking the reputation which Mr. Poe, of all others, esteemed "the precious jewel of his soul."

Yours truly,
C. ALEXANDER.

To Mr. T. C. CLARKE.

According to Mr. Clarke, the "Penn Magazine"
had not been projected at that time, nor indeed
mentioned as in prospect until several years
later.

There is no reputable evidence that Poe ever
quitted his position on the staff of the "Gentleman's" at all; certain it is, that when, in the
latter part of the year 1840, Mr. George R.
Graham, proprietor of "The Casket," purchased
the "Gentleman's Magazine," and merged the
two into one under the title of "Graham's Magazine," Poe was retained as editor. With less restraint upon his pen, and a more liberal business
management, the new magazine speedily gained
in popularity, its subscription list, according to
some accounts, being increased to tenfold of that
of its predecessors, which it combined.

These were, perhaps, the brightest days of the
poet's literary career. Mr. Graham was a congenial companion, sympathetic with Poe's tastes
and aspirations, and, in no small degree, was
able to minister to the material comforts of his
gifted co-laborer. Poe was then in such demand
that, although poorly paid, his industry secured
him a good living; and but for the illness of his

child-wife, upon whom the wasting ravages of her malady had begun to do their work, he would have been happy and comfortable. Griswold has the decency to speak of Poe's home, which he visited at this time, in terms that seem unaccountable coming from this source. He does not neglect a fling at the poet's acknowledged misfortune, but for a Griswoldism the allusion deserves to be admitted here by way of contrast:

"It was while he resided in Philadelphia that I became acquainted with him.

"His manner, except during his fits of intoxication, was very quiet and gentlemanly. He was usually dressed with simplicity and elegance, and when once he sent for me to visit him, during a period of illness caused by protracted and anxious watching at the side of his sick wife, I was impressed by the singular neatness and the air of refinement in his home.

"It was in a small house in one of the pleasant and silent neighborhoods far from the centre of the town, and though slightly and cheaply furnished, everything in it was so tasteful and so fitly disposed that it seemed altogether suitable for a man of genius."

The residence described was a small brick tenement in North Seventh street, in that part of the city then known as Spring Garden.

The house was on the rear portion of the lot, leaving a large vacant space in front, affording Poe and his gentle invalid wife opportunity for indulging their *penchant* for plants and flowers.

"Mr. T. C. Clarke, nearly associated with Poe at this time, writes, "Their little garden in summer, and the house in winter, were overflowing with luxuriant grape and other vines, and liberally ornamented with choice flowers of the poet's selection. Poe was a pattern of social and domestic worth. It was our happiness to participate with them in the occasional enjoyment of the beauty of the flowers, and to watch the enthusiasm with which the fondly attached pair exhibited their floral taste. Here, too, we were wont to participate in the hospitality which always rendered Poe's home the home of his friends. We call to mind some incidents in the pleasantly remembered intercourse that existed between the ladies of our families, especially in the hours of sickness, which rendered so much of Virginia's life a source of painful anxiety to all who had the pleasure of knowing her, and of witnessing the gradual wasting away of her fragile frame.

"But she was an exquisite picture of patient loveliness, always wearing upon her beautiful countenance the smile of resignation, and the warm, even cheerful, look with which she ever greeted her friends.

"How devotedly her husband loved the gentle being, whose life was bound up in his own, is touchingly illustrated in the Griswold description of his visit which I have italicized. '*He sent for me to visit him during a period of illness caused by protracted and anxious watching at the side of his sick wife.*'

"This, coming from the malignant Griswold, is an eloquent tribute to the kindly and tender spirit of Poe, whose devotion no adversity, not even the fiend that haunted him in the fatal cup, could warp or lessen, and this attachment, intense as it was on the part of the poet, was equally strong and enduring in the soul of his 'Annabel Lee,' his gentle mate, whose affection that poem so touchingly and sadly commemorates.

> 'And this maiden, she loved with no other thought
> Than to love and be loved by me.'

"' She was a child,' sings the poem ; and indeed Poe himself was little else in the every-day perplexities and responsibilities of life.   Of Virginia's playful, child-like buoyancy of spirit, I may mention an incident which, though trifling in itself, shows the keen zest with which she enjoyed little trifles which others might have regarded as annoying or impertinent.

"Our little daughter, passing the day with her favorite friend, enlivened the hours with her childish songs.

"There was one which she hinted knowledge of, but positively refused to sing, and it was not until after repeated solicitations from Virginia that the child ventured upon

> 'I never would be married and be called Mistress Poe, Goody
> Poe, &c.

"'Mistress Poe' received the song with peal upon peal of laughter, and insisted, in her exuberance of spirits, on having the homely melody repeated.

"Upon parting, Virginia gave the child a keepsake, which the recipient, no longer a child, now cherishes in memory of the fair and gentle donor.

"On leaving Philadelphia for New York, when breaking up their simple, fairy-like home, we were favored with some of their pet flowers, which, preserved and framed, remain in our household to this day as interesting relics of those happy days with Edgar and Virginia."

During his engagement on "Graham's," which lasted about fifteen months, Poe wrote most of his best stories and many critiques, reviews and essays, fully establishing his reputation as a writer, spite of the fact that most of his writing was far in advance of the age in which he lived, and above the comprehension of the mass of the literary public of that time.

In "Graham's" for April, 1841, appeared "The Murders in the Rue Morgue," the first of those wonderful analytic tales in the conception and evolving of which Poe has never been equalled, although persistently imitated, especially by modern French romancers. This story, indeed, served to introduce the poet to the French public, in a manner that amply justified the author in his frequent charges of plagiarism against his contemporaries.

The anecdote is not new, but it is good enough to bear a repetition in this place.

The author's grotesque conception, as is well known to those who have read the tale, fixes the murder upon a fugitive orang-outang, who had been detected by his master in the act of shaving himself, and escaped with the razor in hand.

One of the Parisian journals, "*La Commerce,*" "cribs" and translates the story from "Graham's" without credit, and it, in turn, is served up as a novelty by a writer in "*La Quotidienne,*" under the appropriate title, "*L'Orang-Otang;*"·a third party incautiously charges "*La Quotidienne*" of a plagiarism from "*La Commerce,*" and in the course of the examination it comes out, that to the American writer only belongs the honor of the composition of the story. "*L'Entr' Acte,*" another Parisian journal, in its issue of the 20th of October, 1846, gave an exceedingly amusing account of the absurd *contretemps* between its contemporaries, complimenting Poe, of whom it speaks as "*un gaillard bien fin et bien spiri-tuel.*"

This controversy naturally resulted in bring-ing Poe's name prominently before the French reading world, and commendatory critiques were at this time published in the "*Revue des Deux Mondes*," and other leading journals, while Madame Isabelle Meunier translated others of his stories for the periodicals. It was reserved for Charles Baudelaire, however, to first discover the poet's genius, and to immortalize it in France by his exquisitely sympathetic and faithful translations. It was Baudelaire, too, who among foreign writers first denounced the mendacities of Griswold, and held him up to the gaze of the French admirers of Poe in his true colors. Speaking of the biographers of Poe, Baudelaire writes, "Some, uniting the dullest unintelligence of his genius to the ferocity of the hypocritical trading class, have insulted him to the uppermost, after his untimely end, rudely hectoring his poor speechless corpse, particularly Mr. Rufus W. Griswold, the *pedagogue vampire*, who has defamed his friend at full length, in an enormous article, wearisome and crammed with hatred, which was prefixed to the posthumous editions of Poe's works. Are there then no regulations in America to keep the curs out of the cemeteries?"

In May, 1841, appeared in the "Saturday Evening Post," of Philadelphia, Poe's celebrated *prophetic* analysis of Dickens' "Barnaby Rudge." From the initial chapters of the story, Poe deduced the entire plot and predicted the actual *dénoûcment.*

Dickens, in his first visit to America, took occasion admiringly to confirm the entire accuracy of the poet's analysis.

Early in 1842 appeared the now famous "Descent into the Maelstrom." In November of the same year "The Mystery of Marie Roget" was published in "Graham's."

The story was another triumph for Poe's analytic power.

This story was founded upon the incident of the murder of a young girl, which took place while Poe was residing in New York. Her death, the poet tells us, occasioned a long-continued excitement, and the mystery attending it had remained unsolved at the period when the story was written and published.

In his note, appended to the edition of his tales published during his lifetime, Poe writes, "'The Mystery of Marie Roget' was composed at a distance from the scene of the atrocity, and with no other means of investigation than the newspapers afforded.

"Thus, much escaped the writer, of which he could have availed himself had he been upon the spot and visited the localities. It may not be improper to record, nevertheless, that the confession of *two* persons (one of them the Madame Delue of the narrative), made at different periods, long subsequent to the publication, confirmed in full, not only the general conclusion, but absolutely *all* the chief hypothetical details by which that conclusion was attained."

Although less satisfactory, as a story, from the fact that the following-out of the clue was for prudential reasons omitted, the "Mystery of Marie Roget," as a representative study of the poet's method, a method flawless in its way, and altogether *sui generis*, it affords a most satisfactory example.

"The Purloined Letter," a sequence to "Marie Roget," and constructed in the same vein, was published shortly afterwards, and "The Premature Burial" appeared at this time.

It was during Poe's connection with "Graham's," too, that he wrote the papers on "Autography," with their prophetic analyses, after the method of Lavater, as well as his papers on "Cryptology," in which he claimed that no cryptograph could be constructed by human ingenuity which human ingenuity could not unravel.

Griswold sneers anent this theory, "a not very dangerous proposition, since it implied no capacity in himself to discover every riddle of this kind that should be invented."

Griswold admits, however, that " he succeeded with several difficult cryptographs that were sent to him."

He does not add that Poe never failed to solve any cryptograph of the enormous number sent to him ; but such is the fact, — a fact which does not excuse the deplorable waste of time and talents upon such a fancy.

But Poe's critical animus frequently carried him beyond the boundaries of reason. He was, unquestionably, lacking in the balance and concentration that would have repressed such profitless deflections, the effect of which is exhibited in the uneven quality of his verse, of which . Oliver Wendell Holmes says, that in the works of no other poet is there exhibited such a difference in quality, as exists between the best and the worst of Poe's poems.

To Poe belongs the honor of discovering and first introducing to the American public the genius of Elizabeth Barrett Browning; and it was at this time, while conducting "Graham's," that many of this author's verses were contributed to its pages.

Shortly after the publication of "The Purloined Letter," in 1842, Poe withdrew from "Graham's" under circumstances which indicate that Griswold's statement that the most friendly relations existed between him and Poe is false, and that the letters published by Griswold as written to him by Poe were fabrications.

Speaking of the severing of Poe's connection with "Graham's Magazine," Dr. Griswold writes, "The infirmities which induced his separation from Mr. White and Mr. Burton at length compelled Mr. Graham to find another editor;" and also in the same connection, "It is known that the personal ill-will on both sides was such that for some four or five years *not a line by Poe was purchased for* 'Graham's Magazine.'" The italics are Dr. Griswold's. He evidently believes with Chrysos, the art-patron in W. S. Gilbert's play of "Pygmalion and Galatea," that when a person tells a lie he "should tell it well."

Mr. Graham, from whom the magazine was named, is now living, and when we last saw him, December, 1873, he was in excellent health. We were then, of course, intent upon securing data in regard to the life of Poe; and in a conversation with Mr. Graham, some peculiarly significant facts touching Griswold's veracity in particular were elicited.

Mr. Graham states that Poe never quarrelled with him; never was *discharged* from "Graham's Magazine;" and that during the "four or five years" italicized by Dr. Griswold as indicating the personal ill-will between Mr. Poe and Mr. Graham, over *fifty* articles by Poe were accepted by Mr. Graham.

The facts of Mr. Poe's secession from "Graham's" were as follows : —

Mr. Poe was, from illness or other causes, absent for a short time from his post on the magazine. Mr. Graham had, meanwhile, made a temporary arrangement with Dr. Griswold to act as Poe's substitute until his return. Poe came

back unexpectedly, and, seeing Griswold in his
chair, turned on his heel without a word, and left
the office, nor could he be persuaded to enter it
again, although, as stated, he sent frequent contributions thereafter to the pages of the magazine.

The following pertinent anecdote, related to us
by Mr. Graham, well illustrates the character of
Poe's biographer. Dr. Griswold's associate in
his editorial duties on "Graham's" was Mr.
Charles J. Peterson, a gentleman long and favorably known in connection with prominent American magazines. Jealous of his abilities, and unable to visit his vindictiveness upon him *in pro-
pria persona*, Dr. Griswold conceived the noble
design of stabbing him in the back, writing under a *nom de plume* in another journal, the "New
York Review." In the columns of the "Review"
there appeared a most scurrilous attack upon Mr.
Peterson, at the very time in the daily interchange
of friendly courtesies with his treacherous associate. Unluckily for Dr. Griswold, Mr. Graham
saw this article, and, immediately inferring, from
its tone, that Griswold was the undoubted author,
went to him with the article in his hand, saying,

" Dr. Griswold, I am very sorry to say I have detected you in what I call a piece of rascality." Griswold turned all colors upon seeing the article, but stoutly denied the imputation, saying, " I'll go before an alderman and swear that I never wrote it." It was fortunate that he was not compelled to add perjury to his meanness, for Mr. Graham said no more about the matter at that time, waiting his opportunity for authoritative confirmation of the truth of his surmises. He soon found his conjectures confirmed to the letter. Being well acquainted with the editor of the " Review," he took occasion to call upon him shortly afterwards when in New York. Asking as a special favor to see the manuscript of the article in question, it was handed to him. The writing was in Griswold's hand.

Returning to Philadelphia, Mr. Graham called Griswold to him, told him the facts, paid him a month's salary in advance, and dismissed him from his post, on the spot.

So it becomes evident that the memory of Poe's biographer, confused upon the point of his discharge from "Graham's," has saddled Poe with

the humiliation and disgrace that alone belonged
to him.

Freed from his responsibilities upon "Graham's," Poe seems to have bent his energies upon
realizing the dream of his life, the establishment
of an independent monthly magazine.   His plans
found favor with influential parties, and a circular
was issued and partially distributed, inviting the
attention of the public to the new enterprise, the
title of which was to be the "Penn Magazine;"
but Poe, spite of his extraordinary analytical
powers, was an inefficient business man, and the
new venture proved but "a flash in the pan," and
the "Penn Magazine" never came to be.   The
idea, however, was still rife in the poet's mind,
and, under different auspices, he again essayed
its realization.

"To have a magazine of his own," writes Hannay, "which he could manage as he pleased,
was always the great ambition of his life.   It was
the chimera which he nursed, the castle in the
air which he longed for, the rainbow of his cloudy
hopes."

Poe invented a new title, selected a motto and
designed a heading, — a copy of which, engraved

from the original drawing by the poet, is given on the next page.

The first public announcement of this new venture, which was to be called "The Stylus," was made in the columns of the "Museum" of Mr. Clarke, Poe's co-partner in the enterprise. We make the following extract, preluding the prospectus of the magazine, which, as embodying the poet's original theories of his ideal magazine, is of sufficient interest to warrant the reproduction here in its entirety : —

"It has often been a subject for wonder that with the pre-eminent success which has attended his editorial efforts, Mr. Poe has never established a magazine, in which he should have more than a collateral interest ; and we are now happy to learn that such is, at length, his intention. By reference to another page of our paper, it will be seen that he has issued the Prospectus of a Monthly, to be entitled "THE STYLUS," for which, it is needless to say, we predict the most unequivocal success. In so saying, we but endorse the opinion of every literary man in the country, and fully agree with Fitz Greene Halleck, that, however eminent may be the contributors engaged, it is, after all, on his own fine taste, sound judgment and great general ability for the task, that the public will place the firmest reliance."

PROSPECTUS OF THE STYLUS.

To be Edited by Edgar A. Poe.

——unbending that all men
Of thy firm TRUTH may say—"Lo! this is writ
With the antique *iron pen*."
—Launcelot Canning.

To the Public.—The Prospectus of a Monthly Journal, to have been called "THE PENN MAGAZINE," has already been partially circulated. Circumstances in which the public have no interest, induced a suspension of the project, which is now, under the best auspices, resumed, with no other modification than that of the title. "The Penn Magazine," it has been thought, was a name somewhat too local in its suggestions, and "THE STYLUS" has been finally adopted.

It has become obvious, indeed, to even the most unthinking,

that the period has at length arrived when a journal of the
character here proposed, is demanded and will be sustained.
The late movements on the great question of International
Copyright are but an index of the universal *disgust* excited
by what is quaintly termed the *cheap* literature of the day, —
as if that which is utterly worthless in itself can be cheap at
any price under the sun.

"The Stylus" will include about one hundred royal-octavo
pages, in single column, per month, forming two thick volumes per year. In its mechanical appearance—in its typogra-
phy, paper and binding — it will far surpass all American
journals of its kind. Engravings, when used, will be in the
highest style of art, but are promised only in obvious illustration of the text, and in strict keeping with the Magazine
character. Upon application to the proprietors, by any agent
of repute who may desire the work, or by any other individual who may feel interested, a specimen sheet will be forward-
ed. As, for many reasons, it is inexpedient to commence a
journal of this kind at any other period than the beginning or
middle of the year, the first number of "The Stylus" will not
be regularly issued until the first of July, 1843.

The necessity for any very rigid definition of the literary
character or aims of "The Stylus" is, in some measure, ob-
viated by the general knowledge, on the part of the public,
of the editor's connection, formerly, with the two most successful periodicals in the country—"The Southern Literary
Messenger" and "Graham's Magazine." Having no propri-
etary right, however, in either of these journals, his objects,
too, being in many respects at variance with those of their
very worthy owners, he found it not only impossible to effect
anything, on the score of taste, for the mechanical appearance

of the works. but exceedingly difficult, also, to stamp upon their internal character that *individuality* which he, believes essential to the full success of all similar publications. In regard to their extensive and permanent influence, it appears to him that continuity, definitiveness, and a marked certainty of purpose are requisites of vital importance; and he cannot help thinking that these requisites are attainable only where a single mind has at least *the general* direction of the enterprise. Experience, in a word, has distinctly shown him — what, indeed, might have been demonstrated *à priori*—that in founding a Magazine wherein his interest should be not merely editorial, lies his sole chance of carrying out to completion whatever peculiar intentions he may have entertained.

In many important points, then, the new journal will differ widely from either of those named. It will endeavor to be, at the same time, more varied and more *unique*,—more vigorous, more pungent, more original, more individual, and more independent. It will discuss not only the Belles-Lettres, but, very thoroughly the Fine Arts, with the Drama; and, more in brief, will give each month a Retrospect of our Political History. It will enlist the loftiest talent, but employ it not always in the loftiest—at least, not always in the most pompous or Puritanical — way. It will aim at affording a fair and not dishonorable field for the *true* intellect of the land, without reference to the mere *prestige* of celebrated names. It will support the general interests of the Republic of Letters, and insist upon regarding the world at large as the sole proper audience for the author. It will resist the dictation of Foreign Reviews. It will eschew the stilted dulness of our own Quarterlies, and while it *may*, if necessary, be no less learned, will deem it wiser to be less anonymous, and difficult to be more dishonest, than they.

An important feature of the work, and one which will be
introduced in the opening number, will be a series of *Critical* and *Biographical Sketches* of *American Writers.* These
Sketches will be accompanied with full-length and characteristic portraits; will include every person of literary note in
America; and will investigate carefully, and with rigorous im-
partiality, the individual claims of each.

It shall, in fact, be the *chief purpose* of "The Stylus" to
become known as a journal wherein may be found, at all
times, upon all subjects within its legitimate reach, a sincere
and fearless opinion. It shall be a leading object to assert
in precept, and to maintain in practice, the rights, while in
effect it demonstrates the advantages, of an absolutely independent criticism;—a criticism self-sustained; guiding itself
only by the purest rules of Art; analyzing and urging these
rules as it applies them; holding itself aloof from all personal bias; and acknowledging no fear save that of outraging
the Right.   CLARKE & POE.

In furtherance of the new enterprise, Poe unfortunately visited Washington. Furnished with
the necessary funds, he supposed that his personal intimacy with the sons of the President, if
not his own talents, would enable him to secure
the names of the members of the Cabinet and
those of other prominent personages in the Capital, with which to place the new literary project
more prominently before the public. But sad
disappointment awaited his cherished hopes.

Felix O. C. Darle

This Agreement,
January, A.D One th
(1843) between Feli
mas C. Clarke with
That the said
ginal designs, or draw
his own composition,
supplied him by Me.
to be employed in th
Stylus", or for other p
agrees to furnish nor
per month, when re
Secondly: Th

Agreement
between
Felix O. C. Darley and Thomas C. Clarke with Edgar A. Poe.

This Agreement, entered into on this Thirty-first day of January, A.D One Thousand, Eight Hundred and Forty-Three (1843) between Felix O. C. Darley, on the one hand, and Thomas C. Clarke with Edgar A. Poe on the other, shows: first:

That the said F. O. C. Darley agrees to furnish original designs, or drawings (on wood or paper as required) of his own composition, in his best manner, and from subjects supplied him by Mess: Clarke and Poe; the said designs to be employed in illustration of the Magazine entitled "The Stylus", or for other purposes. And the said F. O. C. Darley agrees to furnish not less than three of the said designs per month, when required to furnish so many.

Secondly: That Mess: Clarke and Poe agree to demand of Mr Darley not more than five of these designs in any one month, nor these of greater elaboration than the wood-engraving on the first page of the cover of the French edition of "Gil-Blas", as illustrated by Gigoux. And, for each design so furnished, Mess: Clarke and Poe agree to pay the said Darley the Sum of Seven Dollars ($7); the amounts to be paid quarterly, beginning from the date of this Agreement.

Thirdly: That this Agreement is to be valid until the First day of July 1844; and that the said Felix O. C. Darley is hereby required not to furnish, to any Magazine-publisher, any designs of the character described in this Agreement, to be used in any Magazine, within the period during which this Agreement is valid.

In Witness whereof, we, the Undersigned hereunto affix our signatures, this Thirty-first day of January A.D. One Thousand, Eight Hundred and Forty-Three (1843).

Witness, present.   F O C Darley
Henry B. Hirst.   Thos. C. Clarke
Wm D. Ribsan   Edgar A Poe

What harshness. or unsympathetic reception
attended his sanguine expectations was never
definitely known, even by his co-laborer, Mr.
Clarke. That he did not receive the welcome at
the hands of President Tyler that he had rea-
sonably anticipated, is certain, and there is little
reason to doubt that his failure to secure the influential support so essential to his material success was mainly due to the jealous, unappreciative
atmosphere of the politicians among whom he
vainly worked. The spheres of literature and
politics were at that era more antagonistic even
than in the present time; and his delicate, sensitive nature was called upon to receive rebuffs
which only the horny hide of the hack politician
is fitted to bear with equanimity.

In his endeavor to stem the tide of conflicting
circumstances, the poet, forced in Rome to be a
Roman, committed his characteristically fatal
mistake in trusting to a strength which he did not
possess, with the inevitable result, as the following letters to Mr. Clarke only too clearly evidence.

The first is from the poet himself, and its conflicting statements and unsteady penmanship (a
fac-simile of which we give), in which the writ-

er's characteristically clean-cut chirography is
totally unrecognizable, plainly tell the story of
the unfortunate condition of the author.

WASHINGTON, March 11, 1843.

My Dear Sir,— I write merely to inform you of my well-
doing, for, so far, I have done nothing.

My friend Thomas, upon whom I depended, is sick. I suppose he will be well in a few days. In the mean time I shall
have to do the best I can.

I have not seen the President yet.

My expenses were more than I thought they would be, although I have economized in every respect, and this delay
(Thomas being sick) puts me out sadly. *However*, all is
going right. I have got the subscriptions of *all* the departments, President, &c. I believe that I am making *a sensation*
which will tend to the benefit of the magazine.

Day after to-morrow I am to lecture. Rob. Tyler is to give
me an article, also Upsher. Send me $10 by mail as soon as
you get this. I am grieved to ask you for money in this way,
but you will find your account in it twice over.

Very truly yours,
EDGAR A. POE.

THOS. C. CLARKE, Esq.

This was followed, on the succeeding day, by
a letter from Mr. J. E. Dow, at that time editor
of the " Daily Madisonian," a Tyler organ : —

WASHINGTON, March 12, 1843.

Dear Sir,—I deem it to be my bounden duty to write you
this hurried letter in relation to our mutual friend E.A.P.

Washington — March 11. 1843.

My Dear Sir,

I write merely to inform you of my well-doing — so far, I have done nothing. My friend Thomas, on whom I depended, is sick. I suppose he will be well in a few days. In the meantime, I shall have to make the best I can. I have not seen the President yet. My expenses were more than I thought they would be, although I have economised in every respect, and this delay (Thomas' being sick) puts me out sadly. However all is going right. I have got the subscriptions of all the Departments — President, &c &c I believe that I am making a sensation which will tend to the benefit of the Magazine.

Day after to-morrow I am to lecture.

Rob. Tyler is to give me an article also. Please send me $10 by mail, as soon as you get this. I am grieved to ask you for money, in this way. — but you will find your account in it — twice over.

Very truly yours

Edgar A Poe.

Thos. C. Clarke Esq.re

He arrived here a few days since.   On the first evening he seemed somewhat excited, having been over-persuaded to take some Port wine.

On the second day he kept pretty steady, but since then he has been, at intervals, quite unreliable.

He exposes himself here to those who may injure him very much with the President, and thus prevents us from doing for him what we wish to do and what we can do if he is himself again in Philadelphia.   He does not understand the ways of politicians, nor the manner of dealing with them to advantage.   How should he?

Mr. Thomas is not well and cannot go home with Mr. P. My business and the health of my family will prevent me from so doing.

Under all the circumstances of the case, I think it advisable for you to come on and see him safely back to his home. Mrs. Poe is in a bad state of health, and I charge you, as you have a soul to be saved, to say not one word to her about him until he arrives with you.   I shall expect you or an answer to this letter by return of mail.

Should you not come, we will see him on board the cars bound to Phila., but we fear he might be detained in Baltimore and not be out of harm's way.

I do this under a solemn responsibility.   Mr. Poe has the highest order of intellect, and I cannot bear that he should be the sport of senseless creatures who, like oysters, keep sober, and gape and swallow everything.

I think your good judgment will tell you what course you ought to pursue in this matter, and I cannot think it will be necessary to let him know that I have written you this letter;

but I cannot suffer him to injure himself here without giving you this warning.

Yours respectfully,

J. E. Dow.

To Thomas C. Clarke, Esq.,

Philadelphia, Pa.

The enterprise languished from this time, and, like its predecessor in the same path, died ere it was yet born. But whatever may have been the disappointment and chagrin of Poe and his co-laborer Clarke, there was no "quarrel," as stated by Griswold, and reiterated by the poet's London biographer.

Mr. Clarke continued in intimate and friendly relations with the poet.

Apropos of the alleged quarrel, Mr. Clarke writes in a manuscript letter before us, "With Poe I had no quarrel, and I make this statement here because the London editor of his poems, under the influence of Griswold's text, says, 'As a matter of course, he quarrelled and then went to New York.' All this is unjust and ungenerous, and it is painful to see that really magnificent edition of the poems thus disfigured.

"Poor Poe, however harsh he may have been in his vocation of critic, for he was made wretched by any imperfection of art, personally quarrelled with no one, but was a genial, generous friend, invariably kind and gentlemanly to all. How utterly inexcusable in the London editor is the picturing of Poe as deficient in the sense of moral rectitude, and then, after deploring faults that exist only in the editor's imagination and Griswold's mendacities, to attempt, from the poet's writings, to reason us into the belief that all these fancied crimes were the 'legitimate results of an inborn, innate depravity.'

"This goes a step beyond the suggestion of the poet's New York biographer (Griswold) that Poe was 'naturally of an unamiable disposition;' but, as if exulting in the clearness of his own perceptions, the ill-informed critic very complacently concludes that with this key to the character of the poet, there is no difficulty in fully comprehending the strange inconsistencies, the *baseness* and nobleness which his wayward life exhibits. It is deeply to be regretted that any American memoir of the poet should ever have gone forth to the world capable of creating the false estimate, the unjust, because erroneous, impressions which have so prejudiced not only this, but every foreign writer who has undertaken the review of Mr. Poe."

This testimony of one of the few contemporaries of Poe, best calculated by intimate and long-continued association with him to judge, not only of his true character, but of the reliability of the published memoirs of the poet, has a significance that entitles it to an important place in our transcript of the history of Poe's life.

During Poe's connection with Mr. Clarke, he completed an important prose work — a story which was to have been published serially in "The Stylus."

Having expended the money advanced by Mr. Clarke for necessary preliminary expenses, he, upon the failure of the enterprise, left it with his co-partner in the magazine, as security for the amount used until he should be able to reclaim it for subsequent use in his chimerical monthly magazine, the idea of which, upon his part, he had by no means abandoned, as will be evident in later pages of our memoir.

Circumstances, however, combined to prevent its reclamation by the author, and Mr. Clarke, after Poe's death, retained the MSS. of the story,

designing to append it to the memoir of the poet,
which he began but never completed.

Following the failure of "The Stylus," Poe,
in the summer of the same year, 1843, visited
Baltimore, and there made his first appearance
in the rostrum, and on the 25th of the following
November, having returned to Philadelphia for
the same purpose, he came out there in the *rôle*
of lecturer for the first time. Of this performance Mr Clarke writes in "The Museum,"—

"Quite a large, and certainly highly intelligent
audience, attended the lecture on American
Poetry, delivered by Edgar A. Poe, Esq., on
Tuesday evening, before the William Wirt Literary Institute. We have not leisure this week
to give even a brief outline of the lecture, the
character of which may be inferred from the reputation which Mr. Poe has so extensively enjoyed
as a severe and impartial critic. Added to this
important qualification the fact of the lecturer
himself possessing talents as a poet of a high
order, and therefore capable of more truly ap-
preciating his subject, with great analytical power, and that command of language and strength
of voice which enables a speaker to give full ex-

pression to whatever he may desire to say, it will readily be perceived that the lecturer on Tuesday evening combined qualities which are rarely associated in a public speaker. With the exception of some occasional severity, which, however merited, may have appeared somewhat too personal, the lecture gave general satisfaction, especially the portions in which the eloquent sonnets of Judge Conrad, on the Lord's Prayer, were introduced. The judicious reading of these created a marked sensation.

"We hear it suggested that an attempt will be made to prevail on Mr. Poe to re-deliver this lecture in a more central place in the city. With some modification, it would bear repetition, and we dare say, the press will unite in forwarding these views, notwithstanding the cool manner in which Mr. P. laid bare its system of almost universal and indiscriminate eulogy, bestowed alike upon anything and everything — 'from the most elaborate quarto of Noah Webster, down to a penny edition of Tom Thumb.'"

During this year (1843) "The Dollar Magazine" offered a prize of one hundred dollars for a prose story, for which Poe was the successful competitor, offering his ingenious " cipher " tale, " The Gold Bug," which is now probably the most popular of the author's stories in his native country. He also wrote for " Lowell's Pioneer " and other journals.

CHAPTER VI.

CAREER IN NEW YORK.

1844 — 1846.

IN the autumn of 1844, Poe accepted an offer from "The Northern Monthly" to become associate editor of that magazine, and removed to New York. While he was connected with this periodical, his life, giving a brief but faithful sketch of the poet, was published in its columns, with a portrait which did Poe's intellectual head more justice than the caricatures presented in most of the published editions of his works. Griswold makes no mention of this "Life," of the existence of which he must have been aware. It was, we doubt not, too favorable to its subject, to suit the purposes of the falsifier.

The metropolis was not then the great centre for periodical publications that it has come to be now, and Poe found but scanty return for his efforts, while his position was necessarily humbler than that which he had occupied as editor-in-chief of "Graham's."

To eke out his slender means, he accepted, in the autumn of this year, a subordinate position upon "The Mirror," a daily journal conducted by N. P. Willis and George Morris.

The poet Willis, alluding to his connection with "The Mirror," writes,—

"Some four or five years since, when editing a daily paper in this city, Mr. Poe was employed by us, for several months, as critic and sub-editor.

This was our first personal acquaintance with
him. He resided with his wife and mother at
Fordham, a few miles out of town, but was at
his desk in the office from nine in the morning till
the evening paper went to press. With the highest admiration for his genius, and a willingness
to let it atone for more than ordinary irregularity,
we were led by common report to expect a very
capricious attention to his duties, and occasionally
a scene of violence and difficulty. Time went
on, however, and he was invariably punctual and
industrious. With his pale, beautiful and intellectual face as a reminder of what genius was in
him, it was impossible, of course, not to treat him
always with deferential courtesy, and, to our occasional request that he would not probe too deep
in a criticism, or that he would erase a passage
colored too highly with his resentments against
society and mankind, he readily and courteously
assented — far more yielding than most men, we
thought, on points so excusably sensitive. With
a prospect of taking the lead in another periodical, he, at last, voluntarily gave up his employment with us, and through all this considerable
period, we had seen but one presentment of the

Home Journal Office
Nov 12.
dear Poe
I could not find
possibly to go to
concert, but why
you not send the

Home Journal office
Nov 12.

My dear Poe.

I could not find time possibly to go to the concert, but why did you not send the paragraph yourself. You knew of course that it would go in.

I had a letter, not long since, from your sister Enquiring where you were, &, supposing you had mov'd, I could not inform her. You seem as neglectful of your sister as I am of mine, but private letters are "the last ounce that breaks the camel's back" of a literary man.

Yours very truly
N. P. Willis

man — a quiet, patient, industrious and most gentlemanly person, commanding the utmost respect
and good feeling by his unvarying deportment
and ability."*

Poe was engaged upon "The Mirror" for six
months, and during this time, in addition to his
"fag" work upon the paper, he produced several
of his most remarkable works, notably his masterpiece in poetry, "The Raven," which was first published in the February number of "The American
Review," over the *nom de plume* of "Quarles,"
and immediately arrested general attention.

Poe had at this time the *entrée* of the select
social circle of the metropolis, and frequently attended, sometimes with his fair young wife, the
weekly receptions held at the residence of a prominent poetess in Waverly place.   At one of these
soirées, at the request of the accomplished hostess,
he recited "The Raven, " with an effect that fairly
electrified the assemblage.   From this time the
authorship of the poem, of course, became known,
and the laurel leaves of fame were showered
thickly upon the hitherto comparatively unap-
preciated author.

* We give in *fac-simile* an autograph letter written by
Willis to Poe at this time, attesting the kindly, familiar relations existing between them.

Mr. Willis reprinted the poem over Poe's name, and gave it a send-off in the following enthusiastic words: "We regard it as the most effective single example of fugitive poetry ever published in this country, and it is unsurpassed in English poetry for subtle conception, masterly ingenuity of versification, and consistent sustaining of imaginative lift."

Mrs. Browning, in a private letter written a few weeks after its publication in England, says, "This weird writing, this power *which is felt*, has produced a sensation here in England. Some of my friends are taken by the fear of it, and some by the music. I hear of persons who are haunted by the 'Nevermore,' and an acquaintance of mine who has the misfortune of possessing a bust of Pallas cannot bear to look at it in the twilight. Then there is a tale going the rounds of the newspapers about mesmerism,* which is throwing us all into 'most admired disorder'— dreadful doubts as to whether it can be true, as the children say of ghost stories. The certain thing about it is the power of the writer."

One of Poe's relentless biographers, evidently

* "The Facts in the Case of M. de Valdemar."

referring to the source of the inspiration of " The Raven," has presumed recklessly to write that his wife Virginia died a victim to the neglect and unkindness of her husband, " who," he writes, " deliberately sought her death that he might embalm her memory in immortal dirges."

Other writers have reiterated this cruel fabrication, and Gilfillan, fiendishly ascribing to the poet passions controlled by the presence of art until they resembled sculptured flame, writes that he caused the death of his wife that he might have a fitting theme for "The Raven." As the lamented Virginia died more than a year after the publication of "The Raven," this ingenious theory, it appears, rests upon a purely imaginary basis.

As it is well known that Poe was very tenacious of his literary reputation, and acutely appreciative of the honors that belong to fame, it has been deemed not a little remarkable that he should have put forth what he must have known to have been a remarkable poem, anonymously, and at a time, too, when his name was most prominently known to the literary world. But it must be remembered that Poe lived in an epoch

when minds of his stamp were not only not understood nor sympathized with, but were absolutely ridiculed by the world at large.

Of the Americans of this period, Powell, in
his "Living Authors," aptly and ably writes,
"America is jealous of her victories by sea and
land, is proud of advantages with which she has
nothing to do, such as Niagara, the Mississippi,
and the other wonders of nature. An American
points with pride to the magnificent steamboats
which ride the waters like things of life.

"Foreigners sometimes smile at the honest satisfaction, even enthusiasm, which lights up the
national face when a few hundred troops file
down Broadway to discordant drums and squeak-
ing fifes. But all their natural feeling and national pride stops here. So far from the American
public taking any interest in their own men of
genius, in the triumphs of mind, they absolutely
allow others openly to conspire and put down
every attempt to establish a national literature.

"The Americans are a shrewd and far-seeing
people, but they are somewhat too material.
How can America expect her young authors to
vindicate her national glory when she treats them
with indifference and neglect?"

To the constituency so graphically described by Powell, the genius of Poe was forced to address itself or remain silent forever. That he met its cold, hard, unsympathetic reception with the fierce disdain that found its outlet in his scathing criticisms of the typical men of the time, is not to be wondered at, nor is it less surprising that he should shrink from laying bare the secrets of his soul to those so incapable of comprehending their depths.

When, therefore, in his silent vigils, enthralled by the imaginative ecstasy which often possessed and overpowered him, he conceived and wrought out this marvellous inspiration, what wonder is it that his delicate sensibility should prompt him to conceal from the rude gaze of his material audience the secret springs of his inner consciousness, by printing his *chef d'œuvre* over an assumed name, and hedging its origin about with the impenetrable veil of fiction.

Had "The Raven" been, as he described in his paper, "The Philosophy of Composition," a product of art simply, and not of inspiration, his ambition for fame would infallibly have led him, not only to claim the poem openly from the outset, but to have preluded it with the descriptive analysis, using the verse as an illustration of the alleged philosophy of the composition. To his intimates, Poe frequently spoke of the exalted state, which he defined as ecstasy, in which he wrote his poems of imagination. From one of his nearest friends, who knew him in prosperity and adversity, in sickness and health, we learn that none of Poe's romances were more fictitious than his romances about himself and his writings, and his accepted analysis of "The Raven" is confessedly as thorough a specimen of plausible fabrication as is his familiar story of "The Facts in the Case of Monsieur de Valdemar." Like all persons of a highly wrought condition, he resented the slightest approach from the world at large, and from practical people in particular, to the inner citadel of his soul, and he knew well how to use his invincible weapons of defence.

Many admirers of the poet's genius will doubtless prefer that the origin of the inspiration of "The Raven" shall remain enshrouded in the chiaro-oscuro of the mystic suggestiveness of the verse.

But in a much wider circle, there unquestion-

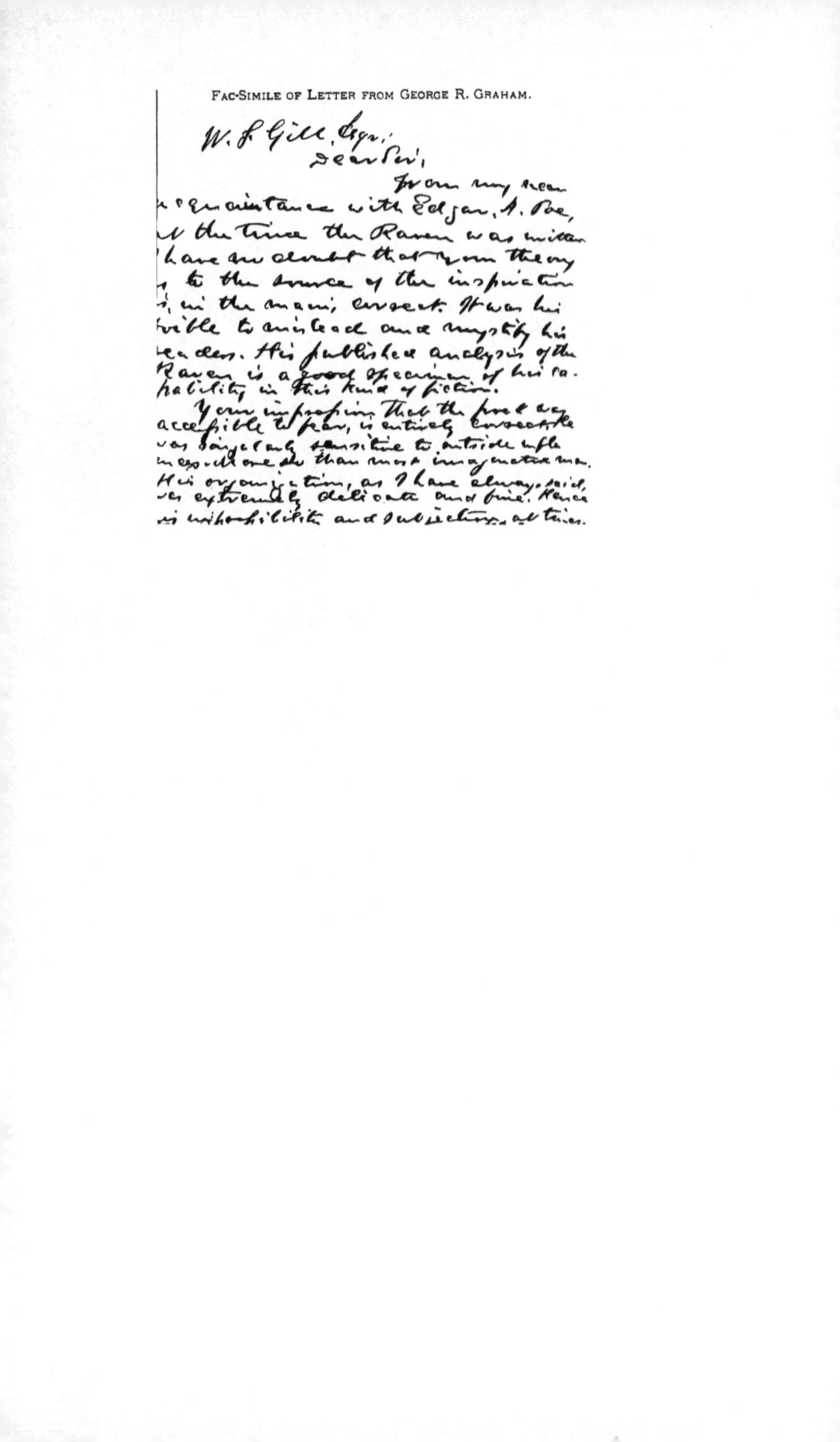

Fac-Simile of Letter from George R. Graham.

W. F. Gill, Esqr.,
    Dear Sir,

From my near acquaintance with Edgar A. Poe, at the time the Raven was written, I have no doubt that your theory as to the source of the inspiration is, in the main, correct. It was his foible to mislead and mystify his readers. His published analysis of the Raven is a good specimen of his capability in this kind of fiction.

Your supposing that the poet was accessible to fear, is entirely correct. He was singularly sensitive to outside influences — more so than most imaginative men. His organization, as I have always said, was extremely delicate and fine. Hence his impressibility and subjection, at times, to influences which would not weigh or fall less weight, with ordinary men. Even when absorbed in writing, I noticed that a sudden breath of air, a jar, a noise unheard by others around him, would startle him. He disliked the dark, and was rarely out at night, when I knew him. On one occasion he said to me, "I believe that Demons take advantage of the night to mislead the unwary" — "although you know," he added, "I don't believe in them."

The mysteries of his inner life, were never fully revealed to any one; but his intimates well understood that to mystify his hearer was a strong element of his mind.

                    Yours very truly
New York May 1st 1877   Geo. R. Graham

ably exists a pardonable desire to learn the true source of this wonderful poem, that, written in any age, in any language, would have given to its author a world-wide fame.

Postulating the opinions which we venture to advance here, upon the result of a process of psychological introversion, which conclusion is confirmed by several of Poe's most intimate acquaintances now living, strengthened by a chain of conclusive circumstantial evidence, we have arrived at a theory of the origin of the poem that has received the approval of Mr. George R. Graham, and others of Poe's friends.

A letter received from Mr. Graham, May 1st, 1877, in this connection, will be read with interest, from the writer's near and friendly intimacy with the poet.

W. F. GILL, ESQ.

DEAR SIR: From my near acquaintance with Edgar A. Poe at the time "The Raven" was written, I have no doubt that your theory as to the source of the inspiration of The Raven is in the main correct. It was his foible to mislead and mystify his readers.

His published analysis of "The Raven" is a good specimen of his capability in this kind of fiction.

Your impression that the poet was accessible to fear, is

entirely correct. He was singularly sensitive to outside influ ences, more so than most imaginative men.

His organization, as I have always said, was extremely delicate and fine. Hence his impressibility, and subjection at times to influences which would not have a feather's weight with ordinary men.

Even when absorbed in writing, I noticed that a sudden breath of air, a noise unheard by others around him, would startle him.

He disliked the dark, and was rarely out at night when I knew him. On one occasion he said to me, "I believe that demons take advantage of the night to mislead the unwary"— "although, you know," he added, "I don't believe in them."

The mysteries of his inner life were never revealed to any one, but his intimates well understood that to mystify his hearer was a strong element of his mind.

Yours very truly,

GEO. R. GRAHAM.

New York, May 1, 1877.

It is a singular fact that Poe's *reading* of "The Raven" in private, was totally at variance with the reading of it as a mere composition.

Had it been constructed, as described by him in his essay on composition, his reading would, unquestionably, have been in accordance with this description, for Poe was too good an elocutionist to fail to adequately voice his conceptions.

As a mere composition, it is impossible to give to the reading of the poem a tithe of the *vrai-semblance* which attaches to it, when rendered according to the theory of its foundation upon an actual experience of the poet.

But for Poe's evident intent to conceal his authorship of the poem, there would be but little expectation of finding any clue to the source of its inspiration. But the fact of the deliberate and exceptional *concealment*, evidences conclusively enough that there was, in the poet's own experience, some basis of fact whereon his imaginative structure was erected.

That some of the most exquisite imaginative fabrics ever constructed have been wrought from the suggestions afforded by some special experience, or by a chance incident or circumstance, there are many familiar examples to demonstrate.

Beethoven's beautiful "Moonlight Sonata" was suggested by a romantic incident during the composer's sojourn at Bonn. Mrs. Julia Ward Howe's "Battle Hymn of the Republic" was a special inspiration which came to her, after witnessing a romantic moonlight march of the troops during the war of the American rebellion.

In seeking for the clue to "The Raven," we find, in recalling the situation of the poet at this time, that he was living at Bloomingdale, New York.

While at this place, and previous to the appearance of "The Raven," his child-wife, Virginia, whom he loved with a purity and intensity that was little short of adoration, was prostrated by a serious illness, which had previously afflicted her, and for weeks her life hung by a thread. Animation was at times, indeed, seemingly suspended, and on one dreary December night, the poet was agonized to find her cold and breathless, apparently dead.

In his lonely, silent vigils in what was, to all intents and purpose, the presence of death, many strange imageries and much bitter self-accusation naturally came to him. Although uniformly kind and tender to his wife, he had been weak and erring from his unfortunate susceptibility to drink, and an exaggerated sense of wrong done to his lost loved one, through his weakness, not unnaturally came to him at this time, exciting the most irrational remorse. His unreasoning, agonized repining, undoubtedly took such complete possession of him as to completely surcharge his mind with the imaginative reveries "that no mortal ever dared to dream before ;" and in picturing to himself his wife as departed, his remorse also forbade him any hope of meeting her in the distant Aidenn of the future. With the added factor of some fugitive bird, or domestic pet (the Poes always kept them) breaking in upon his wild reveries with some slight interruption which the poet's distorted fancy exaggerated into some supernatural visitant, an adequate basis for his masterpiece is found.

That this suggestion of the possible origin of "The Raven" is at least plausible, an analysis of the construction of the poem, coupled with the peculiar characteristics of the poet, will perhaps evidence.

Like many persons of an imaginative, nervous temperament, Poe was susceptible, in certain moods, to a positive sense of the supernatural. This sense he has defined in his letters describing visions suggesting singular fancies.

In his normal state, he did not possess the element of fear ; but when his mind was overwrought to the extent that it frequently was, he was susceptible to impressions that at other times would have affected him very differently.

We find this dread of the supernatural barely hinted at in the first verse, wherein his weariness and loneliness are principally depicted.

The second verse simply describes his isolation, and his sorrow for his lost love. The train of thought inspired by his breathing his hopeless sorrow, is quickly followed by the self-accusation of his remorse for his past, and the vision of an accusing fate dawns upon him, as he recalls the sharp sound that interrupted his loneliness, and strange terrors overcome him.

He is, in fact, beside himself with *fear*, and, as a person in such a state would be likely to do, he endeavors to allay his imaginative dread by ascribing them to some commonplace cause :

"'Tis some visitor entreating entrance at my chamber door,—
Some late visitor entreating entrance at my chamber door :
    This it is, and nothing more."

He nerves himself up to the effort required to throw off his supernatural terror, and opens the door to discover the cause of the noise. He finds nothing but the darkness. His fears, not having been dispelled, as they would have been had he at this time discovered some practical cause for the interruption, are naturally confirmed, and new visions are inspired, and the supposed mysterious visitant takes the form of the spirit of his lost one.

In an ecstasy of dread and excitement, he returns to his lonely watch, only to be again interrupted by a similar noise at the window.

To his delight and surprise, his mysterious visitor takes the welcome form of a truant bird, or some other pet, that has escaped, and returned after the house was closed for the night.

His supernatural dread immediately gives place to a sense of relief at the material presence of. his dumb visitor, and, pacified for the moment, his imaginative fears take flight, and he sits down and merrily chaffs his unexpected guest, glad of any means of occupying his attention and taking his mind off from the morbid imaginings that had possessed it. But under all the would-be blithesome colloquy with his visitor, his fancy will revert to the hopeless dread that has overpowered him, and like the haunted criminal in MM. Erckmann and Chatrian's drama of "The Bells," his imagination coins but one word in answer to his every query; and as Matthias Kant, in the play, is pursued everywhere by the weird jingle of the bells, so the mocking "Nevermore!" seemed to hover in the air, sounding the knell of his lost hopes.

The refrain is not, however, to our mind, invested with any supernatural suggestiveness in the earlier portions of the poem.   Were it so, the poet would have indicated it in the verse.   On the contrary, he writes, —

"Much I marvelled this ungainly fowl to hear discourse so
      plainly,
Though its answer little meaning, little relevancy, bore:"

clearly indicating that his impression was simply one of surprise, not, at first, of fear.

This idea is confirmed in the opening line of the twelfth stanza of the poem :

"But the raven still beguiling all my sad soul into *smiling*,"

which clearly evidences that, up to this point, the impression produced by the appearance of the bird, had not excited any other emotions than the very natural ones of surprise and amusement. But immediately after this, the poet permits himself to do a very hazardous thing for his peace of mind, for he betook himself "*to linking fancy unto fancy,*" until, at the end of the next stanza, we find him just where he was at the beginning, the lighter train of thought suggested by the entrance of his visitor having merged itself in the reminiscences of his lost Lenore, with whom, for the first time in the course of the interview, it occurs to him to connect the bird.

Nothing, it seems to us, is at once so natural and ingenious as the manner of the leading up, in the verse, to this necessary connection of the bird with the subject of the poet's imageries.

The careless, blithesome opening line of the twelfth stanza, already quoted, is in such bold contrast to the sad, closing line of the next stanza that it seems inexplicable that these opposing ideas could have been so congruously reconciled by so simple a device as the deft placing of the "cushioned seat" with its " violet velvet lining."

From this point, the atmosphere of the scene changes, and becomes merged in the supernatural ; the changes of the atmosphere being clearly indicated by the lines, —

"Then methought the air grew denser, perfumed from an
    unseen censer
Swung by seraphim whose foot-falls tinkled on the tufted
    floor."

The bird, no longer a bird to the distorted vision of the poet, assumes to his gaze the shape, first, of an angel, then of an avenging demon.

In one moment of rhapsody, he grasps with frantic joy at the fitful hope of "Nepenthe" for his remorse, only to be cast down to the depths of despair by the re-action which succeeds this still-born hope.

Invested by the poet's fancy with the spirit of prophecy, the bird from that moment assumes to him the form of a Nemesis, and replies to his plaints with the oracular solemnity of a remorseless fate. There are no bounds to the mental anguish depicted in the stanza beginning, —

"Be that word our sign of parting,"

and no limit to the abject despair portrayed in the following, the closing, stanza.

In voicing his imaginary conception in verse, it is not singular that Poe should have selected the raven as typical of his fateful visitor ; for the raven has, for ages past, been renowned as symbolical of ill-omen, and for the purposes of the narration of the story, a *talking* bird was indispensable. What other than the raven could have been effectively employed?

The refrain "Nevermore!" was not less obviously selected, as suggestive, both in sense and sound, of the poet's fateful inspiration.

It will, we think, be conceded that the spontaneity which is an all-pervading characteristic of such of the poems as are *known* to have been inspired by some *actual* person, such as "To Helen," "Annabel Lee" and "For Annie," exists not less palpably in "The Raven." Like these others, it sings itself, to a strange melody, it is true, but not less naturally or truly, and with an exalted beauty of rhythm that seems born of a special inspiration.

The house where "The Raven" was written, stands on a rocky and commanding eminence, a few hundred feet from the corner of Eighty-fourth street and the St. Nicholas boulevard, formerly the Bloomingdale road. It is a plain, old-fashioned, double-framed dwelling, two stories high, with eight windows on each side and one at either gable.

It has a pointed roof, flanked by two tall brick chimneys.

Old and weather-beaten, it now arrests the attention of the passer-by in a neighborhood where most of the houses are of modern construction.

No date can be found for the erection of this quaint building, but it is known that nearly a hundred years ago it gave shelter to General Washington and his officers.

A Mrs. Mary Brennan, who occupied the house for forty-seven years, knew it as bearing a reputation for antiquity before she moved into it.

To Mrs. Brennan it was that Poe, in the early part of the spring of 1844, applied for rooms during the season.

At that time the house was located among the picturesque surroundings of primeval trees, and the beauty of the place had not then been marred by rock-blasting and street-cutting.

Virginia and Mrs. Clemm were, of course, with the poet. They lived together in "The Raven" room during the day, and at night the mother-in-law retired to a small chamber down stairs.

Poe called Virginia "Diddy," and Mrs. Clemm "Muddie." *   They received no visitors, and took their meals in their room by themselves.

---

* Names which Virginia had given to her mother and herself in her childhood.

The House where "The Raven" was written.

The Room where "The Raven" was written.

His landlady recalls the poet as a shy, solitary, taciturn person, fond of rambling alone through the woods or of sitting on a favorite stump of a tree down near the banks of the Hudson River. There she has often observed him gesticulating wildly, and loudly and excitedly soliloquizing. She speaks of him as eccentric, and yet as very quiet and gentlemanly in his manners. He wore, at this time, a small moustache, which he had a habit of nervously twirling.

The " Raven " room had two windows in front, and two at the back, facing the woods.

When not at his favorite seat by the river's brink, he would place himself at one of the front windows, and with Virginia by his side, watch for hours the fading glories of the summer evening skies.

At this time, although engaged upon "The Mirror," and writing for several magazines, his revenues were pitifully small. He was able to pay for his board, but, beyond that, his needs were but scantily met.

The "Raven" room is little altered since the time Poe occupied it. It has a modern mantel-piece, painted black and most elaborately carved.

Poe's name may be found in fine letters cut upon one side of it. His writing-table stood by one of the front windows, and, while seated before it, he could look down upon the rolling waters of the Hudson and over at the Palisades beyond. It was a fitting dwelling for a poet, and though not far from the city's busy hum, the atmosphere of solitude and remoteness was as actual, as if the spot had been in the heart of the Rocky Mountains.

Poe finished "The Raven" in the winter of 1844, and remained with Mrs. Brennan most of the time until the middle of the following summer, when he removed to the city proper.

It is gratifying to be able to record that during the entire period of Poe's stay at this house he carried himself with exemplary correctness, for the reason, undoubtedly, that he was far removed from the social temptations which so frequently beset him in other places.

One of the most amusing Griswoldisms to be found in the reverend doctor's memoir of Poe is his allusion to the public's appreciation of the poet, and to the compensation paid him for his work.

"It is not true," he says, "as has been frequently alleged since Mr. Poe's death, that his writings were above the popular taste, and therefore without a suitable market in this country. His poems were *worth as much* to magazines as those of Bryant and Longfellow (though none of the publishers paid him *half as large a price* for them), and his tales were as popular as those of Willis, who has been commonly regarded as the best magazinist of his time."

Dr. Griswold's parenthesis is as neat a specimen of a Hibernianism as can be instanced. But the doctor's reputation among those who knew him best, was not that of a logician. In fact, a gentleman of the highest culture, a contemporary of Griswold, now living in New York, speaks of him as one of those characters in whom the habit of lying had come to be in such a degree a second nature, as to be excusable on the ground of the falsifier's personal irresponsibility for what was not always a conscious act.

Poe got ten dollars for "The Raven," not, in those times, it would seem, a sum so absolutely insignificant as has been alleged by some of his biographers, for, it must be remembered, it appeared anonymously as originally published.

Still, considering the artistic merits of the poem, the material *quid pro quo* was not munificent, although the author was unquestionably repaid ten-fold in the rich fruits which it brought to him in what was more precious than silver or gold.

The fame which "The Raven" gave to him also justified bringing out a new and improved collection of poems, including his masterpiece, issued by Messrs. Wiley & Putnam, and also two different selections from his " Tales ;" but the prices of books were then so low, and the reading public so limited, that he reaped but little pecuniary advantage from these volumes.

In " Graham's Magazine" for February, 1845, appeared a portrait of Poe, accompanied by a biographical sketch by Professor James Russell Lowell. That this is the ablest and most notable of the many sketches of Poe that have appeared, goes without saying, for no other writer as gifted with every attribute that goes to make the poet and the critic, has ever taken pen in hand in the name and for the weal of Poe.

Of the poet's earlier poems, Professor Lowell writes, "We call them the most remarkable boy-ish poems that we have ever read. We know of none that can compare with them for maturity of purpose and a nice understanding of the effects of the language and metre." Of the lines "To Helen," he says, "The grace and symmetry of the outline are such as few poets ever attain. There is a smack of ambrosia about it."

On his analysis of Poe's genius, Lowell writes,—

"Mr. Poe has two of the prime qualities of genius : a faculty of vigorous, yet minute, analysis, and a wonderful fecundity of imagination. The first of these faculties is as needful to the artist in words, as a knowledge of anatomy is to the artist in colors or in stone. This enables him to conceive truly, to maintain a proper relation of parts, and to draw a correct outline, while the second groups, fills up and colors. Both of these Mr. Poe has displayed with singular distinctness in his prose works, the last predominating in his earlier tales, and the first in his later ones. In judging of the merit of an author, and assigning him his niche among our household gods, we have a right to regard him from our own point of view, and to measure him by our own standard. But in estimating the amount of power displayed in his works, we must be governed by his own design, and, placing them by the side of his own ideal, find how much is wanting. We differ from Mr. Poe in his opinions of the objects of art. He esteems that object to be the creation of beauty, and perhaps it is only in the definition of that word that we disagree with him. But in what we shall say of his writings, we shall take his own standard as our guide. The temple of the god of song is equally accessible from every side, and there is room enough in it for all who bring offerings, or seek an oracle.

"In his tales, Mr. Poe has chosen to exhibit his power chiefly in that dim region which stretches from the very utmost limits of the probable into the weird confines of superstition and unreality. He combines, in a very remarkable manner, two faculties which are seldom found united : a power of influencing the mind of the reader by the impalpable shadows of mystery, and a minuteness of detail which does not leave a pin or a button unnoticed. Both are, in truth, the natural results of the predominating quality of his mind, to which we have before alluded, analysis. It is this which distinguishes the artist. His mind at once reaches forward to the effect to be produced. Having resolved to bring about certain emotions in the reader, he makes all subordinate parts tend strictly to the common centre. Even his mystery is mathematical to his own mind. To him x is a known quantity all along. In any picture that he paints, he understands the chemical properties of all his colors. However vague some of his figures may seem, however formless the shadows, to him the outline is as clear and distinct as that of a geometrical diagram. For this reason Mr. Poe has no sympathy with *Mysticism*. The Mystic dwells *in* the mystery, is enveloped with it; it colors all his thoughts; it effects his optic nerve especially, and the commonest things get a rainbow edging from it. Mr. Poe, on the other hand, is a spectator *ab extrà*. He analyzes, he dissects, he watches

> ——' with an eye serene,
> The very pulse of the machine,'

for such it practically is to him, with wheels and cogs and piston-rods, all working to produce a certain end.

"This analyzing tendency of his mind balances the poetical, and, by giving him the patience to be minute, enables him to throw a wonderful reality into his most unreal fancies. A monomania he paints with great power. He loves to dissect one of these cancers of the mind, and to trace all the subtle ramifications of its roots. In raising images of horror, also, he has a strange success; conveying to us, sometimes by a dusky hint, some terrible *doubt* which is the secret of all horror. He leaves to Imagination the task of finishing the picture, a task to which only she is competent.

> ' For much imaginary work was there;
> Conceit deceitful, so compact, so kind,
> That for Achilles' image stood his spear
> Grasped in an armed hand; himself behind
> Was left unseen, save to the eye of mind.'

"Beside the merit of conception, Mr. Poe's writings have also that of form. His style is highly finished, graceful, and truly classical. It would be hard to find a living author who had displayed such varied powers. As an example of his style, we would refer to one of his tales, 'The House of Usher,' in the first volume of his

'Tales of the Grotesque and Arabesque.' It has
a singular charm for us; and we think that no
one could read it without being strongly moved
by its serene and sombre beauty. Had its author
written nothing else, it would alone have been
enough to stamp him as a man of genius, and
the master of a classic style. In this tale occurs,
perhaps, the most beautiful of his poems.

"The great masters of imagination have seldom resorted to the vague and the unreal as
sources of effect. They have not used dread
and horror alone, but only in combination with
other qualities, as means of subjugating the fancies of their readers. The loftiest muse has ever
a household and fireside charm about her. Mr.
Poe's secret lies mainly in the skill with which he
has employed the strange fascination of mystery
and terror. In this his success is so great and
striking as to deserve the name of art, not arti-
fice. We cannot call his materials the noblest or
purest, but we must concede to him the highest
merit of construction."

Of his abilities as a critic, Lowell says, —

"As a critic, Mr. Poe was æsthetically deficient. Unerring in his analysis of dictions,

metres and plots, he seemed wanting in the faculty of perceiving the profounder ethics of art.
His criticisms are, however, distinguished for
scientific precision and coherence of logic. They
have the exactness, and at the same time the
coldness, of mathematical demonstrations. Yet
they stand in strikingly refreshing contrast with
the vague generalisms and sharp personalities of
the day. If deficient in warmth, they are also
without the heat of partisanship. They are especially valuable as illustrating the great truth,
too generally overlooked, that analytic power is
a subordinate quality of the critic.

"On the whole, it may be considered certain
that Mr. Poe has attained an individual eminence
in our literature which he will keep. He has
given proof of power and originality. He has
done that which could only be done once with
success or safety, and the imitation or repetition
of which would produce weariness."

After six months of service with " The Mirror,"
Poe accepted an offer from Mr. C. H. Briggs to
join him in conducting a new literary gazette,
" The Broadway Journal." He wrote many important criticisms for the columns of "The Broad-

way," among which the more notable were a paper on Mrs. Browning's (then Miss Barrett's) poems, and an essay on plagiarism. The latter was not in his best vein nor his best mood, and, we doubt not, from private letters that we have seen, that he sincerely regretted the animus which he permitted himself to bring to this article.

In March of this year (1845), he delivered his lecture on "The Poets and Principles of Poetry" before the Society Library of New York.

The New England Lyceum had, even at this early period, begun to bud, and the favorable mention of the poet's poetic lecture drew forth an invitation to deliver a poem before the Boston Lyceum.

Apropos of Poe's acceptance of this invitation, and the circumstances incident to its fulfilment. Dr. Griswold devotes considerable space to an elaborate misstatement of the affair. Our lecture managers and lecture public were more exacting twenty-five years ago, on some points, than at the present time. *Now*, it suffices for a reputable celebrity to *show* himself upon the rostrum. Provided he does not occupy too much time (one

hour or an hour and fifteen minutes is about the
fashionable limit), he may be sure of copious applause, of fervent congratulations from beaming
managers, and a plethoric purse upon retiring.
Then, O insatiable manager and exacting public !
the best literary work expressly performed for the
occasion was demanded, or woe betide the celebrity who failed to meet these requirements !

Poe was probably fully conscious of this, and,
not unlike other geniuses in the history of the
literary world, was driven well-nigh frantic in
contemplation of his task of the "written-express-
ly-for-this-occasion poem." It ended as most of
these unequal contests between inspiration and
necessity have ended time and time again. The
day arrived, and no new creations had been
evolved from the goaded and temporarily irre-
sponsive brain. He went to Boston to fill his engagement, nerved to meet the ordeal by a spirit
which brought him compensation for his anxiety,
— a spirit which Mr. E. P. Whipple, the distinguished essayist, at that time immediately associated with Poe, most aptly describes as intellectual mischief. He could not do what he had been
invited to do : well, he would make them believe

that he had filled the demand, if he could, and
then honestly own up, and let them laugh at him
and with him over the *juvenile* poem he gave.

Dr. Griswold makes a labored effort to show
that Poe's failure to meet his engagement to the
letter was due to cares, anxieties, and "feebleness
of will." The charge of feebleness of will, applied to Poe in his strictly literary capacity, is
perhaps one of the most sapient bits of analysis
of which the reverend and profound doctor has
delivered himself. As regards Dr. Griswold's
mention of the assistance of Mrs. Osgood, desired
by Poe, it is so manifestly absurd that the biographer's ingenuity and invention fail to enlist any
credence in this bit of fiction.

The literary world of Boston, twenty-five years
ago, was marked by characteristics that rendered
it anything but liberal and indulgent. Had Poe
had the fortunate tact to disarm his audience by
" owning up " at the outset, and in advance, deftly
knuckling, as he might have done, to its boasted
literary acumen and perceptiveness, all might
have been well. But he chose rather to indulge
his mischievous propensity, to his cost, as it afterwards proved. In his card in " The Broadway

Journal," the poet, in acknowledging his confession to a company of gentlemen at a supper which took place after the reading, truly says, in closing, "We should have waited a couple of days." He should indeed have waited; for among the company was a pitcher that could not contain the water, and the premature leak, being made public, naturally aroused a storm of indignant criticism upon the poet's assumption. His long poem had been applauded to the echo, and the reading of "The Raven" afterwards had sent the audience home in the best of spirits. Poe was too frank and impulsive to keep the joke to himself, and, finding that he had not taken in *all* of the men with brains who received him, he, without a word of solicitation, made a clean breast of it.

The joke was too good to keep. It was very speedily ventilated, and of course got to newspaporial headquarters in a very short time. The poet was accordingly pretty thoroughly scarified by the outraged puritanical press of proper Boston, and had the temerity to reply in the columns of "The Broadway," of which he had become, in October, 1845, the sole proprietor.

His account is worth reproducing, as Griswold has made some special contradictions of the poet's statements, which cannot be permitted to stand. Poe's reply is founded upon a paragraph which appeared in "Noah's Sunday Times," based upon an article in the "Boston Transcript" severely commenting upon "the poem."

"Our excellent friend, Major Noah, has suffered himself to be cajoled by that most beguiling of all beguiling little divinities, Miss Walter, of 'The Transcript.' We have been looking all over her article with the aid of a taper, to see if we could discover a single syllable of truth in it — and really blush to acknowledge that we cannot. The adorable creature has been telling a parcel of fibs about us, by way of revenge for something that we did to Mr. Longfellow (who admires her very much), and for calling her 'a pretty little witch' into the bargain. The facts of the case seem to be these: We *were* invited to 'deliver' (stand and deliver) a poem before the Boston Lyceum. As a matter of course, we accepted the invitation. The audience *was* 'large and distinguished.' Mr. Cushing* preceded us

---

* Hon. Caleb Cushing, then recently returned from his mission to China.

with a very capital discourse.   He was much applauded.   On arising we were most cordially received.   We occupied some fifteen minutes with an
apology for not 'delivering,' as is usual in such
cases, a didactic poem ; a didactic poem, in our
opinion, being precisely no poem at all.   After
some further words — still of apology — for the
'indefiniteness' and 'general imbecility' of what
we had to offer — all so unworthy a *Bostonian*
audience — we commenced, and with many in-
terruptions of applause, concluded.   Upon the
whole, the approbation was considerably more
(the more the pity too) than that bestowed upon
Mr. Cushing.   When we had made an end, the
audience, of course, rose to depart; and about one
tenth of them, probably, had really departed, when
Mr. Coffin, one of the managing committee,
arrested those who remained, by the announcement that we had been requested to deliver 'The
Raven.'   We delivered 'The Raven' forthwith
— (without taking a receipt) — were very cordially applauded again — and this was the end
of it — with the exception of the sad tale invented to suit her own purposes, by that amiable
little enemy of ours, Miss Walter.   We shall

never call a woman ' a pretty little witch ' again as long as we live.

"We like Boston.   We were born there — and perhaps it is just as well not to mention that we are heartily ashamed of the fact.   The Bostonians are very well in their way.   Their hotels are bad.   Their pumpkin pies are delicious.   Their poetry is not so good.   Their common is no common thing — and the duck-pond might answer — if its answer could he heard, for the frogs.   But with all these good qualities, the Bostonians have no soul.   They have always evinced toward us, individually, the basest ingratitude for the services we rendered them in enlightening them about the originality of Mr. Longfellow.

"When we accepted, therefore, an invitation to 'deliver' a poem in Boston, we accepted it simply and solely because we had a curiosity to know how it felt to be publicly hissed — and because we wished to see what effect we could produce by a neat little *impromptu* speech in reply.   Perhaps, however, we overrated our own importance, or the Bostonian want of common civility, which is not quite so manifest as one or two of their editors would wish the public to

believe.   We assure Major Noah that he. is
wrong.   The Bostonians are well-bred, as *very*
dull persons generally are.   Still, with their vile
ingratitude staring us in the eyes, it could scarcely be supposed that we would put ourselves to the
trouble of composing for the Bostonians anything
in the shape of an *original* poem.   We did not.
We had a poem of about five hundred lines, lying by us — one quite as good as new — one, at
all events, that we considered would answer sufficiently well for an audience of Transcendental-
ists.   *That* we gave them; it was the best that
we had for the price, and it *did* answer remarkably well.   Its name was *not* 'The Messenger Star.'   Who but Miss Walter would ever
think of so delicious a little bit of invention as
that?   We had no name for it at all.   The poem
is what is occasionally called a 'juvenile' poem,
but the fact is, it is anything but juvenile now, for
we wrote it, printed it, and published it, in book
form, before we had completed our tenth year.
We read it *verbatim*, from a copy now in our
possession, and which we shall be happy to show
at any moment to any of our inquisitive friends.
We do not, ourselves, think the poem a remark-

ably good one; it is not sufficiently transcenden-
tal. Still it did well enough for the Boston
audience, who evinced characteristic discrimination in understanding, and especially applaud-
ing all those knotty passages which we ourselves
have not yet been able to understand.

"As regards the anger of 'The Boston Times,'
and one or two other absurdities — as regards,
we say, the wrath of Achilles — we incurred it,
or rather its manifestation, by letting some of
our cat out of the bag a few hours sooner than
we had intended. Over a bottle of champagne,
that night, we confessed to Messrs. Cushing,
Whipple, Hudson, Fields, and a few other na-
tives, who swear not altogether by the frog-pond
— we confessed, we say, the soft impeachment
of the hoax. *Et hinc illæ iræ.* We should
have waited a couple of days."

"It is scarcely necessary to suggest," writes
Griswold, "that this must have been written before he had quite recovered from the long intoxication which maddened him at the time to which
it refers; that he was not born in Boston; that
the poem was not published in his tenth year,
and that the 'hoax' was all an after-thought."

That Poe never composed, or was capable of composing, any kind of writing while under the influence of drink, is well known; and that he had his wits about him in this matter, is sufficiently evident from his general adherence, in his reply, to the authenticated facts of the case.

That he was born in Boston, is now universally known to be true, and Griswold could much more readily have substantiated this fact than we, who, like many others, misled by the reckless misstatements of Dr. Griswold, have been obliged, after a lapse of a quarter of a century, to seek for the true facts, which time has not infrequently obliterated. That the hoax was *not* an after-thought, we have Mr. E. P. Whipple's testimony to attest; his account corresponding, as related to us, precisely to that of the poet in his ironical reply to his critics. As to his age when the poem was written, as it has been proved that his other statements were truthful, he should have the benefit of the doubt. There was no plea of illness, as Griswold alleges, as an excuse for delivering the juvenile. It was simply a mischievous conceit upon the part of the poet, which he justified to himself by the contempt in which he held the

Boston public, or, as he termed them, the Frog-pondians, of that period.

Some agreeable reminiscences of the poet's social life at this period, as well as faithful impressions of the character of his intellect, have been given by contemporaries of Poe, whose palmiest days were, undoubtedly, passed in the select literary circles of the metropolis which centred about the home of the prominent authoress to whom we have previously alluded.

The author of the monograph, "Poe and his Critics," writes, quoting from the published comments of a woman of fine genius, prominently known in the social circle in which Poe moved: "It was in the brilliant circles that assembled in the winter of 1845–6 at the houses of Dr. Dewey, Miss Anna C. Lynch, Mr. Lawson and others, that we first met Edgar Poe. His manners were, at these reunions, refined and pleasing, and his style and scope of conversation that of a gentleman and scholar. Whatever may have been his previous career, there was nothing in his appearance or manner to indicate his excesses. He delighted in the society of superior women, and had an exquisite perception of all graces of manner

and shades of expression. He was an admiring
listener and an unobtrusive observer.

" We all recollect the interest felt, at the time,
in anything emanating from his pen ; the relief
it was from the dulness of ordinary writers ; the
certainty of something fresh and suggestive.

" His critiques were read with avidity ; not that
he convinced the judgment, but that people felt
their ability and their courage.   Right or wrong,
he was terribly in earnest."   Mrs. Whitman adds,
"Like De Quincey, he never *supposed* anything
— he always *knew.*

" The peculiar character of his intellect seemed
without a prototype in literature.   He had more
than De Quincey's power of analysis, with a con-
structive nicety and completeness of which the
great English essayist has given no indication."

In evidence of the habitual courtesy and good-
nature noticeable to all who knew him in domestic and social life, the same writer narrates an
incident that occurred at one of the *soirées* to
which we have alluded :   "A lady noted for her
great lingual attainments, wishing to apply a
wholesome check to the vanity of a young author, proposed inviting him to translate for the

company a difficult passage in Greek, of which language she knew him to be profoundly ignorant, although given to rather pretentious display of Greek quotations in his published writings.

"Poe's earnest and persistent remonstrance against this piece of *méchancete*, alone averted the embarrassing test."

As a conversationist, the poet possessed a fascination and individuality that compelled the admiration of all who came within its spell.

Even Dr. Griswold is forced to join hands with the poet's friends in speaking of Poe's matchless gift, and admits that his conversation was at times almost " supra-mortal in its eloquence ;" that " his large and variably expressive eyes looked repose, or shot fiery tumult into theirs who listened, while his own face glowed, or was changeless in pallor, as his imagination quickened his blood or drew it back, frozen, to his heart."

We cannot, from a reading of this photographic drawing of one of the poet's most characteristic traits, refrain from thinking that Griswold really understood Poe more truly than he wrote of him, for, as Mrs. Whitman very aptly says in this connection, " These traits are not the possible accompaniments of attributes which Dr. Griswold has elsewhere ascribed to him."

Of her own impressions of the poet's gift of speech she writes, "The unmatched charm of his conversation consisted in its *genuineness*. As a conversationist we do not remember his equal. We have heard the veteran Landor, called by high authority the best talker in England, discuss with scathing sarcasm the popular writers of the day, convey his political animosities by fierce invectives on 'the pretentious coxcomb Albert* and the cunning knave Napoleon,' or describe in words of strange depth and tenderness the peerless charm of goodness and the naïve social graces in the beautiful mistress of Gore house, 'the most gorgeous Lady Blessington.'

"We have heard the Howadji talk of the gardens of Damascus till the air seemed purpled and perfumed with its roses.

"We have listened to trenchant and vivid talk of the autocrat, to the brilliant and exhaustless colloquial resources of John Neal and Margaret Fuller.

---

* The late Prince Consort of Queen Victoria.

"We have heard the racy talk of Orestes Brownson, in the old days of his freedom and power, have listened to the serene wisdom of Alcott, and treasured up memorable sentences from the golden lips of Emerson.

"Unlike the conversational power evinced by any of these, was the earnest, opulent, unpremeditated speech of Edgar Poe. Like his writings, it presented a combination of qualities rarely met with in the same person; a cool, decisive judgment, a wholly unconventional courtesy and sincere grace of manner, and an imperious enthusiasm which brought all hearers within the circle of its influence."

J. M. Daniel, Esq., United States Minister at Turin,* who knew Poe well at this time, says, "His conversation was the very best we have ever listened to. We have never heard any other so suggestive of thought, or any from which one gained so much. On literary subjects it was the essence of correct and profound criticism divested of all formal pedantries and introductory ideas, the kernel clear of the shell. He was not

---

* 1860.

a brilliant talker in the common after-dinner sense of the word; he was not a maker of fine points or a frequent sayer of funny things. What he said was prompted entirely by the moment, and seemed uttered for the pleasure of uttering it.

"In his animated moods he talked with an abstracted earnestness, as if he were dictating to an amanuensis; and if he spoke of individuals, his ideas ran upon their moral and intellectual qualities, rather than upon the idiosyncracies of their active visible phenomena, or the peculiarities of their manner."

Mrs. Osgood also attests to the matchless charm of his conversation. "But it was in his conversations and his letters," she writes, "far more than in his published poetry and prose writings, that the genius of Poe was most gloriously revealed. His letters were divinely beautiful, and for hours I have listened to him, entranced by strains of such pure and almost celestial eloquence as I have never read or heard elsewhere."

Of his home life, the same writer pens the following exquisite picture : —

"It was in his own simple, yet poetical, home, that to me the character of Edgar Poe appeared in its most beautiful light. Playful, affectionate, witty, alternately docile and wayward as a petted child, for his young, gentle and idolized wife, and for all who came, he had, even in the midst of his most harassing literary duties, a kind word, a pleasant smile, a graceful and courteous attention. At his desk, beneath the romantic picture of his loved and lost Lenore, he would sit, hour after hour, patient, assiduous and uncomplaining, tracing, in an exquisitely clear chirography, and with almost superhuman swiftness, the lightning thoughts — the 'rare and radiant' fancies as they flashed through his wonderful and ever wakeful brain. I recollect one morning toward the close of his residence in this city, when he seemed unusually gay and light-hearted. Virginia, his sweet wife, had written me a pressing invitation to come to them; and I, who never could resist her affectionate summons, and who enjoyed his society far more in his own home than elsewhere, hastened to Amity Street. I found him just completing his series of papers entitled 'The Literati of New York.' 'See,' said he, displaying, in laughing triumph, several little rolls of narrow paper (he always wrote thus for the press), 'I am going to show you, by the difference of length in these, the different degrees of estimation in which I hold all you literary people. In each of these, one of you is rolled up and fully discussed. Come, Virginia, help me !' And one by one they unfolded them. At last they came to one which seemed interminable. Virginia laughingly ran to one corner of the room with one end, and her husband to the opposite with the other. 'And whose lengthened sweetness long drawn out is that?' said I. 'Hear her !' he cried, 'just as if her little vain heart didn't tell her it's herself !'

" During that year," Mrs. Osgood adds, in the same paper, " while travelling for my health, I maintained a correspondence with Mr. Poe, in accordance with the earnest entreaties of his wife, who imagined that my influence over him had a restraining and beneficial effect. It *had*, as far as this, — that having solemnly promised me to give up the use of stimulants, he so firmly respected his promise and me, as never once, during our whole acquaintance, to appear in my presence when in the slightest degree affected by them. Of the charming love and confidence that existed between his wife and himself, always delightfully apparent to me, in spite of the many little poetical episodes in which the impassioned romance of his temperament impelled him to indulge, I cannot speak too earnestly, too warmly."

"The Broadway Journal" proved too heavy a load for the poet's business inexperience to carry, and he was obliged to retire from it, finally, on the third of January, 1846.

"The Literati of New York," mentioned by Mrs. Osgood, as well as some of the poet's tales and sketches, appeared in Godey's "Lady's Book."

These papers made a tremendous local sensation, both in the metropolis and in Philadelphia. Extra editions of the magazine were required to meet the extraordinary demands; the essays were copied far and near, and avalanches of vengeful threats were showered upon the proprietors. In answer to these, Mr. Godey wrote, "We are not to be intimidated by a threat of loss of friends, or turned from our purpose by honeyed words. . . . . Almost every paper that we exchange with has praised our new enterprise and spoken in high terms of Mr. Poe's opinion."

Out of the publication of these papers grew a

fierce discussion between the poet and Thomas
Dunn English, who, like most writers under the
fire of remorseless criticism, lost his temper, and
published, in reply to Poe's original criticism in
the "Literati" series, a malignant and menda-
cious retort, which was copied in "The Mirror,"
and met by the poet with a suit for damages, in
which he recovered several hundred dollars, law
being, at least in this instance, kinder to him than
literature was wont to be.

Griswold indulges in a ground and lofty tumble
on this subject in his memoir.   That is to say, he
deliberately drags the true statement of the affair
in the mire of falsehood, and soars to an altitude
of lying that is venturesome even for him.

Griswold states, after mentioning the fact of
the publication of English's card, that Poe's article was "entirely false in what purported to be
its facts ;" prefixing this statement with another to
the effect that the publication of the "Literati"
led to a disgraceful quarrel, and this to a premature conclusion of the papers.   The facts are, as
may be readily ascertained by referring to the
files of "The Lady's Book," that Poe's critique
of English, which was the second in the "Liter-

ati" series, appeared in the June number, and, far from coming to "a premature conclusion," they ran on, as had been intended, through the following October, while Mr. Godey, with whom we are led to suppose by Griswold, Poe quarrelled, owing to Mr. Godey's declination of his personal reply to Dunn English, accepted all regular contributions from the poet, *whenever he sent them*, and wrote in defence of him in a contemporary magazine of that time.

Those who ascribe Griswold's misstatements regarding Poe simply to his proclivity for lying, should compare the original "Literati" papers, as they appeared in "Godey's," with those in the published edition edited by Griswold. They will then find that a startling discrepancy exists in the *edited* "English" critique, and that the virulent personalities therein appearing, with which Poe is saddled by Griswold, are *entirely* absent from the original review as it appeared in "Godey's."

These papers formed the last important critical work performed by Poe during his residence in the metropolis.

CHAPTER VII.

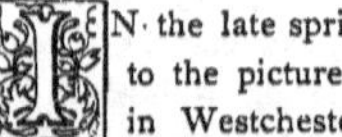IN· the late spring of 1846, Poe removed
to the picturesque locality of Fordham
in Westchester County, New York.
The excitement incident to a residence in the
metropolis had proved injurious to the rapidly
failing strength of his stricken wife, and it was
thought that the pure, free air of the country

home would prove beneficial to the delicate
Virginia.

Some charming descriptions of the poet's home
at Fordham have been given by his contemporaries.

One of these, writing of his first visit there,
says of the place and its inmates, —

"We found him and his wife and his wife's
mother, who was his aunt, living in a little cottage at the top of a hill.

"There was an acre or two of greensward
fenced in about the house, as smooth as velvet
and as clean as the best kept carpet.   There
were some grand old cherry trees in the yard,
that threw a massive shade around them.

"Poe had somehow caught a full-grown bob-
olink.   He had put him in a cage, which he
had hung on a nail driven into the trunk of a
cherry tree.   The poor bird was as unfit to live
in a cage as his captor was to live in the world.
He was as restless as his jailer, and sprang continually, in a fierce, frightened way, from one side
of the cage to the other.   I pitied him; but Poe
was bent on training him.   There he stood, with
his arms crossed, before the tormented bird, his

sublime trust in attaining the impossible, appar
ent in his whole self. So handsome, so impassive
in his wonderful intellectual beauty, so proud and
reserved, and yet so confidentially communica-
tive, so entirely a gentleman, upon all occasions
that I ever saw him, so tasteful, so good a talker,
was Poe, that he impressed himself and his wishes, almost without words, upon those with whom
he spoke.

" On this occasion I was introduced to the young
wife of the poet, and to the mother, then more
than sixty years of age. She was a tall, dignified old lady, with a most lady-like manner, and
her black dress, old and much worn, looked really
elegant on her. She seemed hale and strong,
and appeared to be a sort of universal Providence
for her strange children.

"Mrs. Poe looked very young; she had large
black eyes and a pearly whiteness of complexion
which was a perfect pallor. Her pale face, her
brilliant eyes and her raven hair gave her an un-
earthly look.

" One felt that she was almost a dissolved spirit ;
and when she coughed, it was made certain that
she was rapidly passing away.

MARIA CLEMM.

(From daguerreotype taken in Lowell in 1849.)

"The cottage had an air of taste and gentility that must have been lent to it by the presence of its inmates.

"So neat, so poor, so unfurnished, and yet so charming a dwelling I never saw. The sitting-room was laid with check matting; four chairs, a light-stand and a hanging book-shelf completed its furniture.

"There were pretty presentation copies of books on the little shelves, and the Brownings had a post of honor on the stand. With quiet exultation Poe drew from his side-pocket a letter that he had recently received from Elizabeth Barrett Browning. He read it to us. It was very flattering. . . .

"He was at this time greatly depressed. Their extreme poverty, the sickness of his wife, and his own inability to write, sufficiently accounted for this. We strolled away into the woods, and had a very cheerful time, till some one proposed a game at leaping; I think it must have been Poe, as he was expert in the exercise. Two or three gentlemen agreed to leap with him, and though one of them was tall, and had been a hunter in times past, Poe still distanced them all. But,

In contrast to this specimen of the poet's rugged manliness, is the statement of a near friend of the poet, who writes that Poe was so effeminately sensitive as to be seriously disturbed by the rustle of a silk dress, and would plead with his lady friends to wear stuff that would hang in graceful drapery and make no noise.

Of a later visit, the author from whom we have previously quoted writes: "The autumn came, and Mrs. Poe sank rapidly in consumption, and I saw her in her bed-chamber. The weather was cold, and the sick lady had the dreadful chills that accompany the hectic fever of consumption.

"She lay on the straw bed, wrapped in her husband's great coat, with a large tortoise-shell cat in her bosom. The wonderful cat seemed conscious of her great usefulness. The coat and the cat were the sufferer's only means of warmth, except as her husband held her hands and her mother her feet.

"Mrs. Clemm was passionately fond of her daughter, and her distress on account of her illness and poverty and misery was dreadful to see.

"As soon as I was made aware of these painful facts, I came to New York and enlisted the sympathies and services of a lady whose heart and hand were ever open to the poor and the miserable.

"The lady headed a subscription, and carried them sixty dollars the next week.   From the day this kind lady * first saw the suffering family of the poet she watched over them as a mother.

"She saw them often, and ministered to the comfort of the dying and the living.   Poe," this writer adds, in concluding his impressions and reminiscences, "has been called a bad man. He was his own enemy, it is true, but he was a gentleman and a scholar.   If the scribblers who have snapped like curs at his remains had seen him, as his friends saw him, in his dire necessity and his great temptation, they would have been worse than they deem him, to have written as they have concerning a man of whom they really knew next to nothing."

Griswold, with ferocious cruelty, states that "his habits of frequent intoxication, and his inattention to the means of support, had reduced him

---

* Mrs. Estelle Lewis.

to much more than common destitution ;" when he must have known, or could have readily ascertained from Mrs. Clemm, that his health had been broken by his incessant watching with his sick wife, and he had been unable to get opportunity to make new literary engagements.

The writer from whose reminiscences we have quoted, took the well-meant liberty of making Poe's necessities public without, of course, the poet's knowledge. This mistaken kindness called forth many sympathetic words, however, which showed, Griswold to the contrary, that Poe was not without true friends.

The following paragraph announcing Poe's distress appeared originally in " The New York Express :"—

" We regret to learn that Edgar A. Poe and his wife are both dangerously ill with the consumption, and that the hand of misfortune lies heavy upon their temporal affairs. We are sorry to mention the fact that they are so far reduced as to be barely able to obtain the necessaries of life. This is indeed a hard lot, and we hope that the friends and admirers of Mr. Poe will come promptly to his assistance in his bitterest hour of need."

Mr. Willis, anticipating Mr. Edwin Forrest's plan of a home for disabled members of the dramatic profession, wrote an article favoring the establishment of a home or hospital where educated persons of reduced circumstances might be received and cared for. In it, he says, apropos of Poe's calamities:

"The feeling we have long entertained on this subject has been freshened by a recent paragraph in "The Express," announcing that Mr. Edgar A. Poe and his wife were both dangerously ill, and suffering for want of the common necessaries of life. Here is one of the finest scholars, one of the most original men of genius, and one of the most industrious of the literary profession of our country, whose temporary suspension of labor, from bodily illness, drops him immediately to a level with the common objects of public charity. There was no intermediate stopping-place — no respectful shelter where, with the delicacy due to genius and culture, he might secure aid, unadvertised, till, with returning health, he could resume his labors and his unmortified sense of independence. He must either apply to individual friends — (a resource to which death is sometimes

almost preferable) — or *suffer down* to the level
where Charity receives claimants, but where
Rags and Humiliation are the only recognized
Ushers to her presence. Is this right? Should
there not be, in all highly civilized communities,
an Institution designed expressly for educated
and refined objects of charity — a hospital, a re-
treat, a home of seclusion and comfort, the sufficient claims to which would be such susceptibili-
ties as are violated by the above-mentioned appeal
in a daily newspaper?"

From a letter to Willis, which we quote, the
effect produced upon the proud, sensitive nature
of the poet by the wholesale publication of his
distress will be evident:

My dear Willis, —

The paragraph which has been put in circulation respecting my wife's illness, my own, my poverty, etc., is now lying
before me, together with the beautiful lines by Mrs. Locke,
and those by Mrs. ——, to which the paragraph has given
rise, as well as your kind and manly comments in "The Home
Journal." The motive of the paragraph I leave to the conscience of him or her who wrote it or suggested it. Since the
thing is done, however, and since the concerns of my family
are thus pitilessly thrust before the public, I perceive no mode
of escape from a public statement of what is true and what is
erroneous in the report alluded to. That my wife is ill, then,

is true; and you may imagine with what feelings I add that this illness, hopeless from the first, has been heightened and precipitated by her reception, at two different periods, of anonymous letters — one enclosing the paragraph now in question, the other those published calumnies of Messrs. —— for which I yet hope to find redress in a court of justice.

Of the facts that I myself have been long and dangerously ill, and that my illness has been a well understood thing among my brethren of the press, the best evidence is afforded by the innumerable paragraphs of personal and of literary abuse with which I have been latterly assailed. This matter, however, will remedy itself. At the very first blush of my new prosperity, the gentlemen who toadied me in the old will recollect themselves and toady me again. That I am without friends is a gross calumny, which I am sure you never could have believed, and which a thousand noble-hearted men would have good right never to forgive for permitting to pass unnoticed and undenied. I do not think, my dear Willis, that there is any need of my saying more. I am getting better, and may add, if it be any comfort to my enemies, that I have little fear of getting worse. The truth is, I have a great deal to do; and I have made up my mind not to die till it is done.

Sincerely yours,

December 30, 1846.   '   EDGAR A. POE.

This letter, Griswold charges, was written for effect. Poe, he declares, had not been ill a great while, nor dangerously ill at all; that there was no literary or personal abuse of him in the journals, and that his friends in turn had been applied

to for money until their patience was nearly exhausted. It is needless to say that these statements are, like others by the writer, parts of the
patchwork of falsehood with which the narrative
facts of his memoir of the poet are covered.
That malicious slanders of Poe were published,
the fact of his recovery of heavy damages from
"The Mirror" at a subsequent time, sufficiently
proves; and that he was ill, we have Willis' own
statement, which no one would presume to gain-
say, as proof.

Within a month after the writing of the letter
to Willis, Poe's child-wife died. Although not
now a child, in appearance she was actually girlish, and a portrait which we have seen, taken
after death, while robed for the grave, depicts her
face as one of singular sweetness and purity.
Although her disease was a lingering one, the
face is not wasted nor marked by any lines of
suffering. It seems the face of a child sweetly
sleeping; and, after looking upon it, one does not
wonder at the devoted affection which its living
presence inspired.

No other picture of Virginia is known to be in
existence; and it is to be hoped that at some fu-

ture day the owner of the picture, a sister of the deceased, will waive her present scruples to having the portrait copied, for there is nothing ghastly or deathlike about it. Its atmosphere is that of peace, not of grim death.

Deprived of the companionship and sympathy of his child-wife, the poet suffered what was to him the exquisite agony of utter loneliness.

Night after night he would arise from his sleepless pillow, and, dressing himself, wander to the grave of his lost one, and throwing himself down upon the cold ground, weep bitterly for hours at a time.

The same haunting dread which we have ventured to ascribe to him at the time of his writing "The Raven," possessed him now, and to such a degree that he found it impossible to sleep without the presence of some friend by his bedside when he sought slumber. Mrs. Clemm, his ever-devoted friend and comforter, more frequently fulfilled the office of watcher. The poet, after retiring, would summon her, and while she stroked his broad brow he would indulge his wild flights of fancy to the Aidenn of his dreams. He never spoke nor moved in these moments, unless the hand was withdrawn from his forehead; then he would say, with childish *naïveté*, "No, no, not yet!"—while he lay with half-closed eyes.

The mother, or friend, would stay by him until he was fairly asleep, then gently leave him. He rarely awoke from troubled sleep when his slumbers were thus preluded as he desired; but if, through accident or necessity, he was obliged to seek sleep with no sweet soothings, save the weird conjurings of his own strange fancies, he was invariably distraught and wretchedly uncomfortable.

He continued to reside at Fordham, and the memory of his cherished mate was sacredly preserved in his devoted care of the quaint and pretty little villa with its surroundings of fruit trees and flower beds, and its family of home pets, which to him were, from their associations with his Virginia, as dear as if they had been his children.

Poe had many visitors during his isolated residence at this charming place. An English writer who visited Fordham in the early autumn of 1847, thus described it to Mrs. Whitman:—

"It was at the time bordered by a flower garden, whose clumps of rare dahlias and brilliant beds of fall flowers showed, in the careful culture bestowed upon them, the fine floral taste of the inmates."

An American writer who visted the cottage during the summer of the same year, described it as "half-buried in fruit trees, and as having a thick grove of pines in its immediate neighborhood. Round an old cherry tree, near the door, was a broad bank of greenest turf. The neighboring beds of mignonette and heliotrope, and the pleasant shade above, made this 'a favorite seat.'" "Rising at four o'clock in the morning," writes Mrs. Whitman, "for a walk to the magnificent Aqueduct bridge over Harlem River, our informant found the poet, with his mother, standing on the turf beneath the cherry tree, eagerly watching the movements of two beautiful birds that seemed contemplating a settlement in its branches. He had some rare tropical birds in cages, which he cherished and petted with assiduous care. Our English friend described him as giving to his birds and his flowers a delighted attention that seemed quite inconsistent with the gloomy and grotesque character of his writings. A favorite cat, too, enjoyed his friendly patronage, and often when he was engaged in composition, it seated itself on his shoulder, purring in complacent approval of the work proceeding under its supervision.

"During Mr. Poe's residence at Fordham, a walk to High Bridge was one of his favorite and habitual recreations. The water of the aqueduct is conveyed across the river on a range of lofty granite arches which rise to the height of a hundred and forty-five feet above high-water level. On the top a turfed and grassy road, used only by foot passengers, and flanked on either side by a low parapet of granite, makes one of the finest promenades imaginable. The winding river and the high rocky shores at the western extremity of the bridge are seen to great advantage from this lofty avenue. In the last melancholy years of his life —'the lonesome latter years'— Poe was accustomed to walk there at all times of the day and night, often pacing the then solitary pathway for hours without meeting a human being. A little to the east of the cottage rises a ledge of rocky ground, partly covered with pines and cedars, commanding a fine view of the surrounding country and of the picturesque college of St. John's, which had, at that time, in its neighborhood an avenue of venerable old trees. This rocky ledge was also one of the poet's favorite resorts. Here, through long summer days and through solitary star-lit nights, he loved to sit, dreaming his gorgeous waking dreams, or pondering the deep problems of ' The Universe,' that grand ' prose poem' to which he devoted the last and maturest energies of his wonderful intellect."

The proximity of the railroad, and the great increase of population in the village, have since wrought great changes, and the place would be scarcely recognizable from this description now.

It was during the period of solitariness at Fordham that Poe wrote the mystic "Ulalume;" and, taking into consideration the distraught condition of the poet at this time, it is not singular that, when subjected to Mrs. Whitman's clear-cut analysis, it should be found to be " the most original and weirdly suggestive of all his poems." "It resembles at first sight," says this writer, "some of Turner's landscapes, being apparently 'without form and void, and having darkness on the

face of it.' It is, nevertheless, in its basis, al
though not in the precise correspondence of time,
simply historical."

Such was the poet's lonely midnight walk;
such, amid the desolate memories and sceneries
of the hour, was the new-born hope enkindled
within his heart at sight of the morning star —

      " Astarte's bediamonded crescent —

coming up as the beautiful harbinger of love and
happiness yet awaiting him in the untried future;
and such the sudden transition of feeling, the
boding dread, that supervened on discovering
that which at first had been unnoted, that it shone,
as if in mockery or in warning, directly over the
sepulchre of the lost " Ulalume."

A writer in ".The London Critic " says, quoting
the opening lines of " Ulalume,"—

"These to many will appear only *words;* but
what wondrous words ! What a spell they wield !
What a weird unity is in them ! The instant
they are uttered, a misty picture, with a tarn, dark
as a murderer's eye, below; and the thin yellow
leaves of October fluttering above, exponents of

a misery which scorns the name of sorrow, is hung up in the chambers of your soul forever."

Of the psychal atmosphere of Poe when saturated with the supernaturally imaginative condition, under the spell of which "Ulalume," "The Raven" and "Eureka" were inspired, the author of "Poe and his Critics" writes, "Nothing so solitary, nothing so hopeless, nothing so desolate, as his spirit in its darker moods, has been instanced in the literary history of the nineteenth century."

The poet's extraordinary conceptions of the future were first revealed in the form of a lecture suggestively entitled, "The Universe," delivered before the Society Library of New York city. This was the first of a series of lectures from the proceeds of which Poe expected to realize his long-cherished idea of a monthly magazine of his own, as the following letter to Willis will show : —

FORDHAM, January 22, 1848.

MY DEAR MR. WILLIS, —

I am about to make an effort at re-establishing myself in the literary world, and *feel* that I may depend upon your aid.

My general aim is to start a magazine, to be called "The Stylus;" but it would be useless to me, even when estab-

lished, if not entirely out of the control of a publisher. I
mean, therefore, to get up a journal which shall be *my own*
at all points. With this end in view, I must get a list of at
least five hundred subscribers to begin with, nearly two hundred I have already. I propose, however, to go South and
West, among my personal and literary friends — old college
and West Point acquaintances — and see what I can do. In
order to get the means of taking the first step, I propose to
lecture at the Society Library on Thursday, the 3d of February; and that there may be no cause of *squabbling*, my subject shall *not be literary* at all. I have chosen a broad text,
"The Universe."

Having thus given you *the facts* of the case, I leave all the
rest to the suggestions of your own tact and generosity.

Gratefully, *most* gratefully, your friend always,

EDGAR A. POE.

The subject was sufficiently ponderous to forbid
a large attendance, and the sanguine enthusiast
was obliged to possess his soul with patience,
until opportunity offered for realizing upon his
effort from the publication of the completed work,
which was published not long after by Mr. G. P.
Putnam. The preliminary business negotiation
incident to its publication has been graphically
described by Mr. Putnam. It is worth recalling
in this place.

"I was in his office in Broadway," he states,
"when a gentleman entered, and with a some-

what nervous and excited manner claimed attention on a subject which he said was of the highest
importance. Seated at my desk, and looking at
me a full minute with his 'glittering eye,' he at
length said, 'I am Mr. Poe.' I was 'all ear,' of
course, and sincerely interested. It was the author of 'The Raven,' and of 'The Gold Bug!'
'I hardly know,' said the poet, after a pause,
'how to begin what I have to say. It is a matter
of profound importance.' After another pause,
the poet seeming to be in a tremor of excitement,
he at length went on to say that the publication
he had to propose was of momentous interest.
Newton's discovery of gravitation was a mere
incident compared with the discoveries revealed
in this book. It would at once command such
universal and intense interest that the publisher
might give up all other enterprises, and make
this one book the business of his lifetime. An
edition of fifty thousand copies might be sufficient to begin with; but it would be a small
beginning. No other scientific event in the history of the world approached in importance the
original developments of this book. All this and
more, not in irony or in jest, but in *intense*

earnest—for he held me with his eye like the
Ancient Mariner. I was really impressed, but
not overcome. Promising a decision on Monday
(it was late Saturday P.M.), the poet had to rest
so long in uncertainty upon the *extent* of the edition—partly reconciled, by a small loan, meanwhile. We *did* venture, not upon fifty thousand,
but five hundred."

Although the poet's works are filled, perhaps
unconsciously, with a deep sense of the power
and majesty of Deity, his theory, as expressed
in "Eureka," which he regarded as the crowning
work of his life, of the universal diffusion of
Deity in and through all things, has been regarded as identical with the Brahminical faith as expressed in the "Bagvat Gita." But the closer
criticism of Mrs. Whitman reveals that in the
vast reaches of his thought he arrived at a form
of unbelief that assumes that the central, creative
soul is alternately, not *diffused* only, but merged
and *lost* in the universe, and the universe in it.

"No thinking man lives," he says, "who, at
some luminous point of his life, has not felt himself lost amid the surges of futile efforts at understanding or believing that anything exists

greater than his own soul. The intense, over-
whelming dissatisfaction and rebellion at the
thought, together with the omniprevalent aspirations at perfection, are but the spiritual, coincident
with the material, struggle towards the original
unity. The material *and* spiritual God *now* exists solely in the diffused matter and spirit of the
universe ; and the regathering of the diffused matter and spirit will be but the reconstitution of the
purely spiritual and individual God."

The following ingenious and characteristic
note was found in a copy of the original edition
of "Eureka," purchased at a sale of Dr. Griswold's library. The note, inscribed on the half-
blank page at end of the volume, is in the handwriting of the author :

"Note. — *The pain of the consideration that
we shall lose our individual identity, ceases at
once when we further reflect that the process as
above described is neither more nor less than
that of the absorption, by each individual intelligence, of all other intelligences (that is, of the
universe) into its own. That God may be all in
all, each must become God."*

The publication of "Eureka" naturally aroused

controversy, at a time when sectarian dogmatism and Puritanical narrowness were less tolerant of heretical theories than at the present. A flippant critique of "Eureka" in "The Literary World" drew forth from Poe the following characteristic letter, addressed to the editor, Mr. C. T. Hoffman, that indicated that his many privations had in no way tempered the severity of his powers of criticism when once they were thoroughly aroused : —

Dear sir, — In your paper of July 29, I find some comments on "Eureka," a late book of my own; and I know you too well to suppose for a moment that you will refuse me the privilege of a few words in reply. I feel even that I might safely claim from Mr. Hoffman the right which every author has of replying to his critic, *tone for tone*, that is to say, of answering your correspondent's flippancy by flippancy, and sneer by sneer; but, in the first place, I do not wish to disgrace the "World," and in the second, I feel that I should never be done sneering in the present instance were I once to begin. Lamartine blames Voltaire for the use which he made of misrepresentations (*ruses*) in his attacks on the priesthood; but our young students of theology do not seem to be aware that in defence, or what they fancy to be defence, of Christianity, there is anything wrong in such gentlemanly peccadilloes as the deliberate perversion of an author's text, to say nothing of the minor *indecora* of reviewing a book without reading it and without having the faintest suspicion of what it is about.

You will understand that it is merely the *misrepresentations* of the *critique* in question to which I claim the privilege
of reply; the mere *opinions* of the writer can be of no consequence to me, — and I should imagine of very little to himself — that is to say, if he knows himself personally as well as
I have the honor of knowing him. The first misrepresenta-
tion is contained in this sentence: "This letter is a keen bur-
lesque on the Aristotelian or Baconian methods of ascertain-
ing Truth, both of which the writer ridicules and despises, and
pours forth his rhapsodical ecstasies in a glorification of a
third mode — the noble art of *guessing*." What I *really* say
is this: "That there is no absolute certainty either in the
Aristotelian or Baconian process; that for this reason neither
philosophy is so profound as it fancies itself, and that neither
has a right to sneer at that *seemingly* imaginative process
called Intuition (by which the great Kepler attained his laws),
since 'Intuition,' after all, is but the conviction arising from
those *in*ductions, or *de*ductions, of which the processes are so
shadowy as to escape our consciousness, elude our reason, or
defy our capacity of expression." The second misrepresenta-
tion runs thus: "The developments of electricity and the
formation of stars and suns, luminous and non-luminous,
moons and planets, with their rings, etc., is deduced, very
much, according to the nebular theory of Laplace, from the
principle propounded above." Now, the impression intended
to be made here upon the reader's mind by the " student of
theology " is, evidently, that my theory may be all very well
in its way, but that it is nothing but Laplace over again, with
some modifications that he (the student of theology) cannot
regard as at all important. I have only to say that no gentleman can accuse me of the disingenuousness here implied;

inasmuch as, having proceeded with my theory to that point
at which Laplace's theory *meets it*, I then *give Laplace's
theory in full*, with the expression of my firm conviction of
its absolute truth *at all points*. The *ground* covered by my
theory, as a bubble compares with the ocean on which it
floats ; nor has he the slightest allusion to " the principle propounded above ; " the principle of unity being the source of all
things, the principle of gravity being merely the re-action of
the Divine act which irradiated all things from unity. In fact,
no point of my theory has been even so much as alluded to
by Laplace. I have not considered it necessary here to speak
of the astronomical knowledge displayed in the " stars *and*
suns " of the student of theology, nor to hint that it would be
better grammar to say that "development and formation " *are*
than that development and formation *is*. The third misrep-
resentation lies in a foot-note, where the critic says, "Further
than this, Mr. Poe's claim that he can account for the existence of all organized beings, man included, merely from those
principles on which the origin and present appearance of suns
and worlds are explained, must be set down as mere bold assertion, without a particle of evidence. In other words, we
should term it *arrant fudge*." The perversion of this point
is involved in a wilful misapplication of the word " principles." I say " wilful," because at page 63 I am *particularly*
careful to distinguish between the principles proper, attraction and repulsion, and those merely resultant *sub*-principles
which control the universe in detail. To these sub-principles,
swayed by the immediate spiritual influence of Deity, I leave,
without examination, all that which the student of theology
so roundly asserts I account for on the principles which account for the constitution of suns, etc. .   .

Were these "misrepresentations" (*is* that the name of them?) made for any less serious a purpose than that of branding my book as "impious," and myself as a "pantheist," a "polytheist," a Pagan, or a God knows what (and, indeed I care very little, so it be not a "student of theology"), I would have permitted their dishonesty to pass unnoticed, through pure contempt for the boyishness, for the *trun-down-shirt-collarness* of their tone; but as it is, you will pardon me, Mr. Editor, that I have been compelled to expose a "critic" who, courageously preserving his own *anonymosity*, takes advantage of my absence from the city to misrepresent, and th is villify me, *by name.*

EDGAR A. POE.

Fordham, September 20, 1848.

In July, 1848, Poe visited Lowell, Massachusetts, and there delivered his lecture on Poetry. Another visit to this city, in the spring of 1849, was eventful in that, during the time he remained there, at the house of a dear friend, he composed and finished his greatest descriptive poem, "The Bells," a study of which he had previously made and sent to "Sartain's Magazine."

Commenting on the wonderful contrast presented between the study and the finished masterpiece, the editor of "Sartain's" gives the following, including a copy of "The Bells," as originally composed : —

"The singular poem of Mr. Poe's, called 'The Bells,' which we published in our last number, has been very extensively copied. There is a curious piece of literary history connected with this poem, which we may as well give now as at any other time. It illustrates the gradual development of an idea in the mind of a man of original genius. This poem came into our possession about a year since. It then consisted of *eighteen lines!* They were as follows : —

THE BELLS. — A SONG.

The bells! — hear the bells!
The merry wedding bells!
The little silver bells!
How fairy-like a melody there swells
From the silver tinkling cells
Of the bells, bells, bells!
Of the bells!

The bells! — ah, the bells!
The heavy iron bells!
Hear the tolling of the bells!
Hear the knells!
How horrible a monody there floats
From their throats—
From their deep-toned throats!
How I shudder at the notes
From the melancholy throats
Of the bells, bells, bells!
Of the bells!

For every sound that floats
From out their ghostly throats
    Is a groan.
    And the people — ah, the people
    Who live up in the steeple

        All alone,
And who, tolling, tolling, tolling,
    In that muffled monotone,
Feel a glory in so rolling
    On the human heart a stone —
They are neither man nor woman —
They are neither brute nor human,
But are pestilential carcases disparted from their souls —
        Called Ghouls : —
    And their king it is who tolls : —
And he rolls, rolls, rolls, rolls
    A Pæan from the bells !
And his merry bosom swells
    With the Pæan of the bells !
    And he dances and he yells ;
Keeping time, time, time,
In a sort of Runic rhyme,
    To the Pæan of the bells —
        Of the bells : —

"About six months after this, we received the poem enlarged and altered nearly to its present size and form; and about three months since, the author sent another alteration and enlargement, in which condition the poem was left at the time of his death."

The original MSS. of "The Bells," in its enlarged form, from which the draft sent to "Sartain's" was made, is in our possession at this time. The interlinings and revisions are peculiarly interesting as showing the author's extraordinary care in fine points of versification.

In the twelfth line of the first stanza of the original draft, the word "bells" was repeated *five* times, instead of four, as Poe printed it, and but twice in the next line. In changing and obviously improving the effect, he has drawn his pen through the fifth repetition, and added another, *underlined*, to the two of the next line.

The same change is made in the corresponding lines in the next stanza.

In the sixth line of the third stanza, the word "much" is placed before "too," with the usual mark indicating the transposition which he made in printing it, and as originally written the word "anger," in the fifth line from the last in this stanza, was written "clamor," while "anger" was placed in the last line. By the transposition of these, he gained the euphonious alliterative effect in the last line which would otherwise have been wanting.

In the sixth line of the fourth stanza, the word "meaning" was first used in lieu of the more impressive "menace," to which it gave place. The eighth line of this stanza was first written, "From out their ghostly throats;" and the eleventh line was changed twice, reading first, "Who live up in the steeple," then "They that sleep" was substituted for "who live," and finally "dwell" was printed instead of "sleep."

After the eighteenth line, a line was added that was elided entirely in the poem as printed. It read, —

"But are pestilential carcasses departed from their souls."

The ideality of the poem is immeasurably improved by the elision of this repulsive thought. In making the change, omitting this line, he simply substituted, "They are ghouls," in the next line, in pencil.

A *fac simile* of a portion of this fourth stanza, which we give, showing some of the important alterations, is, perhaps, the most interesting specimen of the poet's hand that has been printed.

Some informal but quite suggestive recollections of the poet have been given us by a lady now living, at that time a school-girl in her teens. According to this lady's statement, — and she is certainly disinterested, — the poet does not seem to have been the moral wreck that some of his biographers have sought to make him appear.

·"I have in my mind's eye a figure somewhat below medium height, perhaps, but so perfectly proportioned, and crowned with such a noble head, so regally carried, that to my girlish apprehension he gave the impression of commanding stature. Those clear, sad eyes seemed to look from an eminence rather than from the ordinary level of humanity, while his conversational tone was so low and deep that one could easily fancy it borne to the ear from some distant height.

·"I saw him first in Lowell, and there heard him give a lecture on Poetry, illustrated by readings. His manner of rendering some of the selections

constitutes my only remembrance of the evening
which so fascinated me.   Everything was rendered with pure intonation and perfect enuncia-
tion, marked attention being paid to the rhythm.
He almost *sang* the more musical versifications.
I recall more perfectly than anything else the un-
dulations of his smooth baritone voice as he
recited the opening lines of Byron's 'Bride of
Abydos,'—

'Know ye the land where the cypress and myrtle
Are emblems of deeds that are done in their clime,'—

measuring the dactylic movement perfectly as if
he were scanning it.   The effect was very pleasing.

"He insisted strongly upon an even, metrical
flow in versification, and said that hard, unequally
stepping poetry had better be done into prose.   I
think he made no selections of a humorous character, either in his public or parlor readings.   Indeed, anything of that kind seems entirely incom-
patible with his personality.   He smiled but seldom, and never laughed, or said anything to
excite mirth in others.   His manner was quiet
and grave.   John Brown of Edinboro' might
have characterized it as "lonely."   In thinking

of Mr. Poe in later years I have often applied
to him the line of Wordsworth's Sonnet, —

' Thy soul was like a star, and dwelt apart.'

"I did not hear the conversation at Mrs. Richmond's after the lecture, when a few persons
came in to meet him; but I remember that my
brother spoke with enthusiasm of the elegance
of Mr. Poe's demeanor and the grace of his conversation.   In alluding to it he always says, 'I
have never seen it equalled.'   A lady in the
company differed from Mr. Poe, and expressed
her opinions very strongly.   His deference in
listening was perfect, and his replies were models
.of respectful politeness.   Of his great satirical
power his pen was generally the medium.   If he
used the polished weapon in conversation, it was
so delicately and skilfully handled that only a
quick eye would detect the gleam.   Obtuseness
was always perfectly safe in his presence.

"A few months later than this, Mr. Poe came
out to our home in Westford.   My recollections
of that visit are fragmentary, but vivid.

"During the day he strolled off by himself 'to
look at the hills,' he said.   I remember standing

in the low porch with my sister as we saw him
returning ; and as soon as he stepped from the
dusty street on to the greensward which sloped
from our door, he removed his hat and came
to us with uncovered head, his eyes seeming
larger and more luminous than ever with the ex-
hilaration of his walk.   I recall his patiently un-
winding from a nail a piece of twine that had
been carelessly twisted and knotted around it,
and then, hanging it back again over the nail in
long, straight loops.   It was a half-unconscious
by-play of that ingenious mind which deciphered
cryptographs, solved enigmas of all kinds, and
wrote 'The Gold Bug' and 'The Balloon Hoax.'
My memory photographs him again sitting before
an open wood fire in the early autumn evening,
gazing intently into the glowing coals, holding
the hand of a dear friend, while for a long time
no one spoke, and the only sound was the ticking
of the tall clock in the corner.   I wish I knew
what he was dreaming about during that rapt
silence.

Later in the evening he recited, before a little
reading club, several of his own poems, one of
Willis', commencing, 'The shadows lay along

Broadway,' which, he said, was a special favorite with him; and one or two of Byron's shorter
pieces. I thought everything was perfect; but
others said that much more effect might be given
to his own unique poems. I suppose his voice
and manner expressed the 'Runic rhyme' better
than the 'tintinnabulation' or the 'turbulency'
of the 'bells, bells, bells.' That poem was then
fresh from the author's brain, and we had the
privilege of hearing it before it was given to the
world.

"The next morning I was to go to school; and
before I returned he would be gone. I went to
say good-bye to him, when, with that gracious,
ample courtesy of his, which included even the
rustic school-girl, he said, 'I will walk with you.'
He accompanied me nearly all the way, taking
leave of me at last in such a gentle, kindly manner that the thought of it brings tears now to the
eyes that then looked their last upon that finished
scholar, and winning, refined gentleman."

In 1845, Poe had visited Providence on
his way to deliver his poem before the Boston
Lyceum; and there, while wandering through
a retired street, he saw, walking in her garden,

Mrs. S. H. Whitman, to whom, in his lecture on Poetry, he had awarded " a preëminence in refinement of art, enthusiasm, imagination and genius." The romantic incident of his meeting with Mrs. Whitman has, as is generally known, been exquisitely described by him in the poem " To Helen."

Dr. Griswold's citation of the lines in connection with one of his most scandalous anecdotes, has given them a celebrity which even their sumptuous beauty might not otherwise have insured to them.

Early in September, 1848, the poet, having obtained a letter of introduction to Mrs. Whitman, again visited Providence, and made her acquaintance. Notwithstanding some opposition from the relatives of the lady, they were subsequently engaged.

The lack of all moral sense has been so universally imputed to Poe by his biographers, that the following passages from a letter by the poet, one of a series addressed to his *fiancée*, in which he speaks for himself upon this subject, may be worthy of consideration in this place :

OCTOBER 18th.

. . . Of what avail to me in my deadly grief are your enthusiastic words of mere admiration! You do not love me, or you would have felt too thorough a sympathy with the sensitiveness of my nature to have so wounded me, as you have done, with this terrible passage of your letter: "How often I have heard men and even women say of you, 'He has great intellectual power, but no principle, no moral sense.'" Is it possible that such expressions as these could have been repeated to me — to me — by one whom I loved — ah, whom I *love!* And you ask me why such opinions exist. You will feel remorse for the question, when I say to you that until the moment when those horrible words first met my eye, I would not have believed it possible that any such opinions could have existed at all; but that they do exist, breaks my heart in separating us forever. I love you too truly ever to have offered you my hand, ever to have sought your love, had I known my name to be so stained as your expressions imply. . . . It is altogether in vain that I tax my memory or my conscience. There is no oath which seems to me so sacred as that sworn by the all-divine love I bear you. By this love, then, and by the God who reigns in heaven, I swear to you that my soul is incapable of dishonor; that with the exception of occasional follies and excesses, which I bitterly lament, but to which I have been driven, and which are hourly committed by others without attracting any notice whatever, I can call to mind no act of my life which would bring a blush to my cheek or to yours. If I have erred at all in this regard, it has been on the side of what the world would call a Quixotic sense of the honorable, of the chivalrous. The indulgence of this sense has been the true voluptuousness of my life. It was for this species of luxury that in early youth I deliberately threw away a large fortune rather than endure a trivial wrong. . . . Ah, how profound is my love for you, since it forces me into these egotisms, for which you will inevitably despise me!

But grant that what you urge were even true, do you not feel in your inmost heart of hearts that the soul-love of which the world speaks so often, and so idly, is, in this instance at least, but the veriest, the most absolute of realities?

Ah. I could weep, I could almost be angry with you, for the unwarranted wrong you offer to the purity, to the sacred reality, of my affection.

Referring to another passage in the letter quoted above, the poet writes:—

"May God forever shield you from the agony which these words occasion me!"

You will never know, you can never picture to yourself, the hopeless, rayless despair with which I now trace these words. . . .

Nevertheless, I must now speak to you the truth or nothing. . . . But alas! for nearly three years I have been ill, poor, living out of the world, and thus, as I now painfully see, have afforded opportunity to my enemies to slander me in private society, without my knowledge, and thus with impunity.

Although much may, however (and I now see must), have been said to my discredit during my retirement, those few who, knowing me well, have been steadfastly my friends, permitted nothing to reach my ears, unless in one instance, where the accusation was of such character that I could appeal to a court of justice for redress.

I replied to the charge fully in a public newspaper, suing "The Mirror" (in which the scandal appeared), obtaining a verdict and recovering such an amount of damages as for the time to completely break up that journal. And you ask why men so misjudge me, why I have enemies!

If your knowledge of my character, and of my career, does not afford you an answer to the query, at least it does not become me to suggest the answer. Let it suffice that I have had the audacity to remain poor that I might preserve my independence; that, nevertheless, in letters, to a certain extent and in certain regards, I have been successful; that I have been a critic, an unscrupulously honest, and no doubt in many cases, a bitter one.

That I have uniformly attacked, where I attacked at all, those who stood highest in power and influence, and that, whether in literature or in society, I have seldom refrained from expressing, either directly or indirectly, the pure contempt with which the pretensions of ignorance, arrogance or imbecility inspire me. And you who know all this, you ask me why I have enemies. Ah, I have a hundred friends for every individual enemy; but has it ever occurred to you that you do not live among my friends?

Had you read my criticisms generally, you would see why all those whom you know best know me least and are my enemies. Do you not remember with how deep a sigh I said to you in ——, "My heart is heavy, for I see that your friends are not my own!" . . . Forgive me, best and beloved ——, if there is bitterness in my tone. Towards you there is no room in my soul for any other sentiment than devotion. It is fate only which I accuse. — It is my own unhappy nature.

Further on in this letter, the poet draws this picture of his ideal home : —

"I suffered my imagination to stray with you, and with the

few who love us both, to the banks of some quiet river in
some lovely valley of our land. Here, not too far secluded
from the world, we exercised a taste controlled by no conven-
tionalities, but the sworn slave of a Natural Art, in the building for ourselves a cottage which no human being could ever
pass without an ejaculation of wonder at its strange, weird
and incomprehensible, yet simple, beauty. Oh, the sweet and
gorgeous, but not often rare, flowers in which we half-buried
it — the grandeur of the magnolias and tulip-trees which stood
guarding it — the luxurious velvet of its lawn — the lustre of
the rivulet that ran by its very door — the tasteful yet quiet
comfort of its interior — the music — the books — the unos-
tentatious pictures — and, above all, the love, the love that
threw an unfading glory over the whole! — Alas! all is now
a dream."

This letter of eloquent protest and appeal bears
date October 18, 1848. No engagement at the
time subsisted between the parties.

Shortly after its date an incident occurred
which has been widely chronicled as "an outrage on the eve of an appointed marriage."

Mrs. Whitman has permitted us to publish her
own clear and authentic statement of the facts
which underlie this scandal, thereby placing the
story in its true light, and imparting a profound interest to the fragment of a letter to
which she alludes, and of which we present

for the terrible agony which I have so lately endured — an agony known only to my God and to myself — seems to have passed my soul through fire and purified it from all that is weak. Henceforward I am strong :— this those who love me shall see — as well as those who have so relentlessly endeavored to ruin me. It needed only some such trials as I have just undergone, to make me what I was born to be . by making me conscious of my own strength . —

FAC-SIMILE OF LETTER TO MRS. WHITMAN.

a *fac-simile* copy. Later, a conditional engagement was made. The poet was not able to
adhere to the conditions, and the lady was, in
duty and honor to her family, bound to give up
the alliance.

But it was not broken under any such circumstances as those fabricated by Dr. Griswold in
his narration of the affair in his memoir. As
this misstatement of Griswold is probably the
most malicious of all his published mendacities,
we have taken special pains to gather the evidence of its falsity; evidence that Griswold deliberately suppressed, although most of it was
published previous to his issue of his memior of
Poe in a permanent form. The correspondence
which we quote, principally comprises letters from
Wm. J. Pabodie, Esq., a prominent lawyer of
Providence, very intimately acquainted both with
Poe and with Mrs. Whitman, at the time of their
engagement.

To the editors of the "New York Tribune,"
Mr. Pabodie writes, after the misstatements of
Griswold had been published and repeatedly
copied by various perodicals:

"In an article on American Literature in the 'Westminster

Review' for April, and in one on Edgar A. Poe, in 'Tait's Magazine' for the same month, we find a repetition of certain incorrect and injurious statements in regard to the deceased author, which should not longer be suffered to pass unnoticed. These statements have circulated through half a dozen foreign and domestic periodicals, and are presented with an ingenious variety of detail. As a specimen, we take a passage from Tait, who quotes as his authority Dr. Griswold's memoir of the poet :

"' Poe's life, in fact, during the three years that yet remained to him, was simply a repetition of his previous existence, notwithstanding which, his reputation still increased, and he made many friends. He was, indeed, at one time, engaged to marry a lady who is termed "one of the most brilliant women in New England." He, however, suddenly changed his determination ; and after declaring his intention to break the match, he crossed, the same day, into the city where the lady dwelt, and, on the evening that should have been the evening before the bridal, " committed in drunkenness such outrages at her house as made necessary a summons of the police."'

"The subject is one which cannot well be approached without invading the sanctities of private life ; and the improbabilities of the story may, to those acquainted with the parties, be deemed an all-sufficient refutation. But in view of the rapidly increasing circulation which this story has obtained, and the severity of comment which it has elicited, the friends of the late Edgar A. Poe deem it an imperative duty to free his memory from this unjust reproach, and to oppose to it their unqualified denial. Such a denial is due, not only to the memory of the departed, but also to the lady whose home is supposed to have been desecrated by these disgraceful outrages.

"Mr. Poe was frequently my guest during his stay in Providence. In his several visits to the city I was with h m daily. I was acquainted with the circumstances of his engageme ..., and with the causes which led to its dissolution. I am authorized to say, not only from my personal knowledge, but also from the statements of all who were conversant with the affair, that there exists not a shadow of foundation for th stories above alluded to.

"Mr. Poe's friends have no desire to palliate his faults, nor to conceal the fact of his intemperance — a vice which, though never habitual to him, seems, according to Dr. Griswold's published statements, to have repeatedly assailed him at the most momentous epochs of his life. With the single exception of this fault, which he has so fearfully expiated, his conduct, during the period of my acquaintance with him, was invariably that of a man of honor and a gentleman; and I know that, in the hearts of all who knew him best among us, he is remembered with feelings of melancholy interest and generous sympathy.

"We understand that Dr. Griswold has expressed his sincere regret that these unfounded reports should have been sanctioned by his authority; and we doubt not, if he possesses that fairness of character and uprightness of intention which we have ascribed to him, that he will do what lies in his power to remove an undeserved stigma from the memory of the departed.

"WILLIAM J. PABODIE.

"Providence, June 2, 1852."

In answer to this, we find Dr. Griswold, in the *rôle* of a bully, impudently attempting to put

down Mr. Pabodie's dignified statement *vi et
armis*.   He writes to Mr. Pabodie a private letter, as follows : —

New York, June 8, 1852.

Dear Sir,— I think you have done wrong in publishing
your communication in yesterday's "Tribune" without ascer-
taining how it must be met.   I have never expressed any
such regrets as you write of, and I cannot permit any statement in my memoir of Poe to be contradicted by a reputable
person, unless it is shown to be wrong.   The statement in
question I can easily prove, on the most unquestionable
authority, to be true; and unless you explain your letter to
"The Tribune" in another for publication there, you will
compel me to place before the public such documents as will
be infinitely painful to Mrs. Whitman and all others concerned.
The person to whom he disclosed his intention to break off
the match was Mrs. H——t.   He was already engaged to
another party.   I am sorry for the publication of your letter.
Why you did not permit me to see it before it appeared, and .
disclose in advance these consequences, I cannot conceive.   I
would willingly drop the subject, but for the controversies
hitherto in regard to it, with which you are acquainted.   Before writing to "The Tribune" I will await your opportunity
to acknowledge this note, and to give such explanations of
your letter as will render any public statement on my part
unnecessary.

In haste, yours respectfully,

R. W. Griswold.

W. J. Pabodie, Esq.

To this insolent and impotent letter, which was

tesselated with scandalous and irrelevant stories respecting Mr. Poe's relations with some of his esteemed and valued friends, Mr. Pabodie replied by calmly reiterating his published statement in "The New York Tribune," and by adducing further proof of Griswold's audacious fabrications. The tone of this letter is in striking contrast to that of Griswold's virulent and threatening note. Its forbearing mildness, indeed, renders it open to criticism on this ground.

JUNE 11, 1852.

Mr. RUFUS W. GRISWOLD.

Dear Sir, — In reply to your note, I would say that I have simply testified to what I know to be true, namely, that no such incident as that so extensively circulated in regard to certain alleged outrages at the house of Mrs. Whitman, and the calling of the police, ever took place. The assertion that Mr. Poe came to Providence the last time with the intention of breaking off the engagement, you will find equally unfounded, when I have stated to you the facts as I know them. In remarking that you had expressed regret at the fact of their admission into your memior, I had reference to a passage in a letter written by Mrs. H. to Mrs. W., which was read to me by the latter some time since. I stated in all truthfulness the impression which that letter had left upon my mind. I enclose an extract from the letter, that you may judge for yourself:

"Having heard that Mr. Poe was engaged to a lady of

Providence I said to him, on hearing that he was going to that city, ' Mr. Poe, are you going to Providence to be married?'—'I am going to deliver a lecture on Poetry,' he replied.   Then, after a pause, and with a look of great reserve, he added, 'That marriage may never take place.'" *

I know that from the commencement of Poe's acquaintance with Mrs. W. he repeatedly urged her to an immediate marriage.   At the time of his interview with Mrs. H., circumstances existed which threatened to postpone the marriage indefinitely, if not altogether to prevent it.   It was, undoubtedly, with reference to these circumstances that his remark to Mrs. H. was made; certainly not to the breaking-off the engagement, as his subsequent conduct will prove.   He left New York for Providence on the afternoon of his interview with Mrs. H., not with any view to the proposed union, but at the solicitation of the Providence Lyceum; and on the evening of his arrival, delivered his lecture on American Poetry, before an audience of some two thousand persons. During his stay he again succeeded in renewing his engagement, and in obtaining Mrs. W.'s consent to an immediate marriage.

He stopped at the Earl house, where he became acquainted with a set of somewhat dissolute young men, who often invited him to drink with them.   We all know that he sometimes yielded to such temptations, and on the third or fourth evening after his lecture, he came up to Mrs. Whitman's in a state of partial intoxication.   I was myself present nearly the

---

* In another letter Mrs. H. writes, referring to this conversation, indignant at the use which Dr. Griswold had made of these innocent words, more than a year after she had reported them, " These were Mr. Poe's words, and these were all."

whole evening, and do most solemnly affirm that there was no noise, no disturbance, no "outrage," neither was there any "call for the police." Mr. Poe said but little. This was undoubtedly the evening referred to in your memoir, for it was the only evening in which he was intoxicated during his last visit to this city; but it was not "the evening that should have been before the bridal," for they were not then published, and the law in our State required that they should be published at least three times, on as many different occasions, before they could be legally married.

The next morning Mr. Poe manifested and expressed the most profound contrition and regret, and was profuse in his promises of amendment. He was still urgently anxious that the marriage should take place before he left the city.

That very morning he wrote a note to Dr. Crocker, requesting him to publish the intended marriage at the earliest opportunity, and entrusted this note to me, with the request that I should deliver it in person. You will perceive, therefore, that I did not write unadvisedly in the statement published in "The Tribune."

For yourself, Mr. Griswold, I entertain none other than the kindest feelings. I was not surprised that you should have believed those rumors in regard to Poe and his engagement; and although, from a regard for the feelings of the lady, I do not think that a belief in their truth could possibly justify their publication, yet I was not disposed to impute to you any wrong motive in presenting them to the public. I supposed rather that, in the hurry of publication and in the multiplicity of your avocations, you had not given each statement that precise consideration which less haste and more leisure would have permitted. I was thus easily led to believe, from Mrs.

H.'s letter, that ·upon being assured of their incorrectness, and upon learning how exceedingly painful they were to the feelings of the surviving party, you sincerely regretted their publication. I would fain hope so still.

In my article in " The Tribune," I endeavored to palliate their publication on your part, and to say everything in your extenuation that was consistent with the demands of truth and justice to the parties concerned. I would add, in regard to Poe's intoxication on the evening above alluded to, that to all appearances it was as purely accidental and unpremeditated as any similar act of his life. By what species of logic any one should infer that, in this particular instance, it was the result of a malicious purpose and deliberate design, I have never been able to conceive. The facts of the case, and his subsequent conduct, prove beyond a doubt that he had no such design.

With great respect,
Your obedient servant,
WILLIAM J. PABODIE.

Rev. RUFUS W. GRISWOLD.

It will be seen by this correspondence that the attempt of Dr. Griswold to browbeat Mr. Pabodie was courteously but firmly and unanswerably met. Dr. Griswold never paid the slightest attention to this letter, contenting himself with leaving on record the outrageous scandal that has since obtained an almost unprecedented circulation in the numerous memoirs of Poe, based upon Dr. Griswold's malicious invention, that have

been published. The introduction of the story
of the banns would seem to come under the head
of what lawyers call "an accessory after the
fact." Dr. Griswold had probably heard that
the banns were written, if not published, and
took advantage of this information to adroitly
garnish his story with them. To set this question
at rest forever, we have obtained permission to
quote the following passages of a letter received
from Mrs. Whitman in August, 1873:

"No such scene as that described by Dr. Griswold ever trans-
pired in my presence. No one, certainly no woman, who
had the slightest acquaintance with Edgar Poe, could have
credited the story for an instant. He was essentially and in-
stinctively a gentleman, utterly incapable, even in moments
of excitement and delirium, of such an outrage as Dr. Griswold has ascribed to him. No authentic anecdote of coarse
indulgence in vulgar orgies or bestial riot has ever been recorded of him. During the last years of his unhappy life,
whenever he yielded to the temptation that was drawing him
into its fathomless abyss, as with the resistless swirl of the
maelstrom, he always lost himself in sublime rhapsodies on
the evolution of the universe, speaking as from some imaginary platform to vast audiences of rapt and attentive listeners.
During one of his visits to this city, in the autumn of 1848, I
once saw him after one of those nights of wild excitement,
before reason had fully recovered its throne. Yet even then,
in those frenzied moments when the doors of the mind's

"Haunted Palace" were left all unguarded, his words were
the words of a princely intellect overwrought, and of a heart
only too sensitive and too finely strung. I repeat that no one
acquainted with Edgar Poe could have given Dr. Griswold's
scandalous anecdote a moment's credence.

> "Yours, etc.,
>
> "S. H. WHITMAN."

Apropos of Mr. Griswold's professed friendship
for Poe, which he endeavors to demonstrate in
copies of a correspondence which I cannot refrain
from thinking was extensively "doctored" by the
doctor, to suit his purpose, we are able to present,
perhaps not inappropriately in this place, an extract from an autograph letter of Dr. Griswold,
written to Mrs. Whitman in 1849.

The object of this was evidently to cool Mrs.
Whitman's friendship for Mrs. Clemm, thus pre-
venting their further intimacy. This was desirable to Dr. Griswold for evident reasons.

NEW YORK, December 17, 1849.

MY DEAR MRS. WHITMAN.

I have been two or three weeks in Philadelphia, attending
to the remains which a recent fire left of my library and furniture, and so did not receive your interesting letter in regard
to our departed acquaintance until to-day. I wrote, as you
suppose the notice of Poe in "The Tribune," but very hastily.

on the e
persiste
refutat
too late

Mr Poe
injustic
house —
farewel
the city
In th
State of
one of o
& alton

or the idle story of outrages committed
of an appointed marriage — Since
lumny & misstatement call for direct
— let me speak explicitly before it is

n the afternoon of November 8, 1848,
ronded by some imaginary sense of
wrong, abruptly left my mother's
nt me a note of renunciation and
owing his intention of immediately leaving
engagement at the time existed between us.
orning he returned to the house in a
delirium. Dr. A. H. Okie, then, as now,
ost eminent physicians, was sent for
ing an hour in his presence advised his
he house of his friend, Wm J Pabodie,
s most kindly cared for until his recovery.
as not the phrensy of violence & outrage
l desolation & despair, calling forth
est sympathy of those who witnessed
as after this incident & shortly before
turn to Fordham that I consented
onal engagement, whose conditions
less to say he had already lost
o fulfil.
ment of a letter written soon after his
csimile of which you have recently seen.
do all the letters written during our
ment, the agony of the conflict, in which
oomed to defeat—with a power which no
could heighten

I was not his friend, nor was he mine, as I remember to have told you. I undertook to edit his writings to oblige Mrs. Clemm, and they will soon be published in two thick volumes, of which a copy shall be sent to you. I saw very little of Poe in his last years. . . . I cannot refrain from begging you to be very careful what you say or write to Mrs. Clemm, who is not your friend, nor anybody's friend, and who has no element of goodness or kindness in her nature, but whose heart and understanding are full of malice and wickedness. I confide in you these sentences for your own sake only, for Mrs. C. appears to be a very warm friend to me. Pray destroy this note, and at least act cautiously, till I may justify it in a conversation with you.

> I am yours very sincerely,
> RUFUS W. GRISWOLD.

This brief note affords a tolerably good specimen of the utter duplicity of the man. In his printed memoir of Poe, he quotes a correspondence indicating professed friendship; in private, he unequivocally owns that no friendship ever existed between Poe and himself.

He writes that Mrs. Clemm is a friend to no one, and stigmatizes her character; and in the same breath speaks of her warm friendship for him.

Had Griswold lived in Othello's time, no one could have disputed with him the position of " mine ancient," honest Iago.

While living at Fordham, at this time, Poe is said to have written a book entitled "Phases of American Literature."

Mr. M. A. Daly has stated that he saw the complete book; but as nothing is known as to the fate of the manuscript, it is to be inferred that Dr. Griswold, who, of course, had charge of all of Poe's literary papers, found it desirable, to escape further scarifying, to destroy it.

In the summer of 1849, the poet quitted Fordham, and returned to Richmond, partly for the purpose of delivering his lectures, and partly to accept an engagement on "The Southern Literary Messenger," to which the whirligig of time thus brought him back, to end the work he had begun twelve years before. For "The Messenger," at this time, he wrote his sharp paragraphic papers, "Marginalia," a few poems and several reviews, among which were reviews of Mrs. Osgood and Mrs. Lewis (Stella). With the exception of a brief visit to Philadelphia, he remained in and about Richmond for several months, making his headquarters at the office of "The Messenger."

The editor of "The Messenger" at that time,

the late J. P. Thompson, has related not a few
anecdotes of his acquaintance with Poe during
his latter days

One of these we recall in connection with one
of his truest and most beautiful poems.

Poe had completed his engagement with "The
Messenger," and had called to take leave of
Mr. Thompson. He was about to take a trip
North for Mrs. Clemm, to bring her South. He
was needy, and had asked Mr. Thompson for a
loan of five dollars to help out his travelling expenses.

As he was about to go, he turned to Mr.
Thompson, saying, "By the way, you have been
very kind to me,—here is a little trifle that may
be worth something to you;" and he handed
Mr. Thompson a small roll of paper, upon which
was written the exquisite lines of "Annabel Lee."

During this same season, Poe had apparently
had better luck than had been his fortune in
former times, in obtaining material guarantees
for starting "The Stylus," and as late as August
in this year, had formed definite plans with Mr.
E. H. N. Patterson, for issuing the magazine in
July of the following year.

The following letter from Mr. Patterson indicates that definite plans had been formed. It is interesting as being the last allusion anywhere to be found of this fated enterprise of the sanguine but unfortunate poet :

OQUAWKA, Ill., Aug. 21, 1849.

EDGAR A. POE, Esq.

My Dear Sir, — Yours of the 7th inst. was received last night, and I hasten to reply. I am truly glad to hear that you are recovering your health, and trust it will soon be fully restored. You cannot enter into the joint publication of a $3 Mag. with " your heart in the work." Well, what say you to this ? —

In publishing a $5 magazine, of 96 pp., monthly, — page same size as "Graham's," — in bourgeois or brevier (instead of long primer and brevier, as first proposed), it would be necessary for me to make an outlay of at least $1100 (this amount including a supply of paper for three months for 2000 copies). Now, if you are sure that, as you before thought, 1000 subscribers can be obtained who will pay upon receipt of the first number, then you may consider me pledged to be with you in the undertaking.

If this proposition meets your approval, you may immediately commence your journey to St. Louis — making easy stages through the South, and operating on your way — so as to reach that city by the middle of October (say the 15th), keeping me advised of your progress, as you proceed, by letter, say every two weeks. I will meet you at St. Louis, by the time mentioned, at which time I shall be more at leisure than before, and can then settle on arrangements. You may associate my name with your own in the matter, the same as if I had met you in person.

Adopt your own title. I leave this matter to you, as belonging peculiarly to your department. (Remember, however, published simultaneously at New York and St. Louis.) The first number can be issued in July — it is now too late to do it in January, and it would not be advisable to commence at any time other than the beginning or the middle of the year. I will try to be at St. Louis on the 15th of October, if your answer to this be favorable; until which time I bid you Godspeed, and beg leave to sign myself,

Most truly yours,

ED. II. N. PATTERSON.

P.S. — I send this via St. Louis and Vincennes, and will make a duplicate via Chicago to-morrow.

Yours,   E. H. N. P.

One of the saddest pictures of Poe's later days, when the dark mantle of a blighting sorrow was enshrouding him, is afforded in an account, which is gathered from an old-time associate of the poet, of his last visit to Philadelphia, which took place at this time. The picture is none the less sad in that some of the poet's happiest hours had been passed in his cosy little home in that city, years before, with his charming and devoted child-wife, Virginia.

During this visit, which was made only a

short time previous to his death in Baltimore,
Poe was an inmate of the hospitable mansion
of the artist and publisher, Mr. J. Sartain, widely
known as the proprietor of "Sartain's Magazine,"
whose kindness the poet had frequently shared.
Fortunate, indeed, would it have been for Poe
had he met with this staunch friend on first
reaching the city at this time. Had he fallen
into his protecting hands earlier, instead of meeting with reckless associates, ready as in old times
to tempt him to the indulgence inevitably fatal to
him, how different might have been his fate.I
But it was ordained otherwise. When he finally
reached the residence of his kind friend, Poe
was in a highly excited condition, almost dis-
tracted indeed. His mind seemed bewildered
and oppressed with the dread of some fearful
conspiracy against his life; nor could the argu-
ments or entreaties of his friend convince him
that some deadly foe was not, at that very moment, in pursuit of him. He begged for a razor
for the purpose of removing the mustache from
his lip, in order, as he suggested, that he might
disguise his appearance, and thus baffle his pur-
suers. But, unwilling to place such an instru-

ment in his hands, he was prevailed upon to allow his host to effect the desired change upon which he imagined his safety depended. The condition of Poe's mind was such, that Mr. Sartain, after persuading him to lie down, remained watching with him through the night with anxious solicitude, unwilling to lose sight of the unfortunate sufferer for a moment. The following night, Poe insisted upon going out. He turned his steps towards the River Schuylkill, accompanied, however, by his devoted friend, whose apprehension was strengthened by the vehemence with which, without cessation, he poured forth, in the rich, musical tones for which he was distinguished, the fervid imageries of his brilliant but over-excited imagination. The all-absorbing theme which still retained possession of his mind, was the fearful conspiracy that threatened his destruction. Vainly his friend endeavored to re-assure and persuade him. He rushed on with unwearied steps, threading different streets, his companion striving to lead him homeward, but still in vain.

Towards midnight, they reached Fairmount, and ascended the steps leading to the summit,

Poe all the while giving free scope to the conversational powers for which he was always remarkable, insisting upon the imminence of his peril, and pleading with touching eloquence for protection.

In the darkness of the night, the solemn stillness only broken by the even fall of the water below, in peaceful contrast with the wild disorder of the unhappy poet's brain, he seemed a personification of the subject of his own "Raven,"—

"Deep into that darkness peering, long I stood there, wondering, fearing, doubting, dreaming,
Dreaming dreams no mortal ever dared to dream before."

He did not recover from this intense excitement until, subsequently escaping from the house, he wandered out into the neighborhood of the city, and, throwing himself down in the open air in a pleasant field, his shattered nerves found a comfortless but sorely needed repose.

He awoke refreshed; but, like Cassio, "remembered a mass of things, but nothing distinctly."

All that he could recall to mind were the entreaties and persuasions of some "guardian angel," who had sought to dissuade him from a frightful purpose. He recalled the kind remonstrances, but nothing more,—not even the identity of the friend to whose kind offices he had been indebted. The next day, his friend parted with him, and, as fate ordained, forever.

While in Richmond, Poe had renewed his acquaintance with Mrs. Shelton, to whom he had paid attentions in his youth, and before he left "The Messenger," they had become engaged.

When he left Richmond, it was with the intention of going North to bring Mrs. Clemm from Lowell, to attend his marriage with Mrs. Shelton.

At Baltimore, he had the misfortune to meet a friend at the depot who persuaded him to drink. He accepted, with the usual result—actual mental derangement, to a degree that at Havre de Grace, the conductor of the train, finding him in a state of delirium, and knowing that he had friends and relatives in Baltimore, brought him back to that city. He arrived at night. It was the eve of a municipal election, and as he was still partially deranged, wandering through the streets, he was seized by the ruffianly agents of one of the political clubs, and locked up for the night for use at the polls in the morning.

The next day he was taken out, still in a state of delirum, drugged, and made to repeat votes at eleven different wards.

The following day he was found in the back room of one of the political headquarters, and removed to the Washington University Hospital, situated on Broadway, north of Baltimore street.

What wonder that an organization as sensitive as his, should have succumbed to the terrible exposure and humiliation which had been his lot at the hands of the brutal wretches among whom he had unwittingly fallen. The exposure, combined with the effects of liquor and drugs, had brought on an inflammation of the brain, and shortly after midnight of the 7th of October, 1849, the unfortunate man breathed his last, surrounded by the few friends and relatives whom it had been possible to notify during the day.

Mr. Neilson Poe, his cousin, his nearest living male relative, was with him in his last moments, and took charge of his papers after his death.

J. J. Moran, M.D., attended the poet at the hospital. During the conversation that passed between the physician and his patient, Dr. Moran asked, wishing to ascertain whether he would be inclined to take liquor, "Will you take some wine?" "He opened wide his large eyes," writes Dr. Moran, "and fixed them so steadily upon me, and with such anguish in them, that I looked from him to the wall beyond the bed, while he said, 'Sir, if its potency would transport me to the Elysian bowers of the undiscovered spirit world, I would not taste it, — I would not taste it. Of its horrors who can tell?'" His last coherent words, as recalled by Dr. Moran, were, "It's all over; write 'Eddie is no more.'"* He had previously directed that letters be written to Mrs. Shelton, at Norfolk, Virginia, and to Mrs. Clemm, at Lowell, Mass., acquainting them with his illness.

He was buried on the 8th of October, in the burial ground of the Westminster Church, near the corner of Fayette and Greene streets, Baltimore.

For months previous to his untimely death, Poe had been carefully abstemious, up to the last week, during which his misfortunes in Philadelphia and Baltimore occurred; and the sudden and fearful change, from the most careful and tender

------

* "Eddie" was the name which Mrs. Clemm called him by.

nursing, to the most reckless exposure to the damp and cold of an out-of-doors bed, produced immediate effeçts, planting the insidious seeds that flowered into deadly bloom, with the aid of his later unfortunate exposure when in the hands of the Baltimore roughs.

We are prone to accept the *most obvious* explanation of an event as the true explanation or cause of that event. The lesson of experience teaches us that the most obvious analyses are, as a rule, the most deceptive. It is commonly believed, for instance, that Edgar Poe died from the effects of dissipation, which, *gradually*, from long continuance, undermined his constitution. We are convinced that his death is not to be assigned to any such positive and debasing cause. For many years of his lifetime, spite of all accounts to the contrary, he lived happy and comfortable, in a charming home, with a companion that realized his delicate and refined ideal. The shadow of the destroying angel's hand that first cast its blight upon this companion, was the one great, unlooked-for sorrow that he could not, would not, accept unrepiningly.

From the moment of his wife's death, he waged an unequal battle with a relentless fate. Well

knowing his need — the balance and support afforded by the interchange of spiritual sympathy
with a congenial mind — he was deprived even
of the possible gratification of this want· by the
peculiar construction of his mental organism.

The Upas of his morbid imagination, no longer
controlled by the healthful restraints of the pure,
simplicity of the atmosphere that his child-wife
had thrown around him, twined like a poisonous
blight about him, enervating his nobler energies,
and, spite of his reason, blasting the healthier
aspirations of his genius.

Poe may be regarded as a man who lived and
died never entirely understood; — one who, sensitive to a degree altogether incomprehensible to
practical minds, yet was so unfortunate as to live
among the practical-minded only, and at a time
when temperament, as such, was essentially
omitted in society's estimate of a man. It was
Poe's misfortune that his temperament was totally
at variance with the spirit of the age in which he
lived.

In a certain sphere of thought, his ideas were
altogether in advance of those of the people with
whom he was associated. The world at large
was never responsive to him in any significant de-

gree. It could admire or despise him. It could not sympathize with him, or appreciate him

The nineteenth century, generous as it has been in the production of geniuses, has been none too prolific in these rare creations. Many of them, alas, now live only in memory and in their works.

It behooves us then to preserve their memories free from baleful calumny. The veil of calumny has heavily clouded the memory of Edgar Allan Poe.

May we be permitted to hope that, from the facts and impressions which our researches, which claim not to be adequate or complete, have enabled us to give, some rays of light may find their way through the repelling gloom that has, in the past, shut out from view much of the fairer side of the poet's life.

THE END.

APPENDIX.

APPENDIX.

FROM a correspondence with Mrs. Clemm, who, there can be no reasonable doubt, is correctly described by Willis as " one of those angels upon earth that women in adversity can be," we find the most positive testimony that Dr. Griswold's association with collecting the works of Poe, and of writing a memoir of the author, was purely voluntary and speculative.

It presents simply the fact of a designing and unscrupulous man, prompted by hatred and greed of gain, taking advantage of a helpless woman, unaccustomed to business, to defraud her of her rights, and gratify his malice and his avarice at her expense.

A small sum having been given. to Mrs. Clemm in exchange for Poe's private papers, Dr. Griswold draws up a paper for Mrs. Clemm to sign, announcing his appoinment as Poe's literary executor, not omitting, of course, a touching allusion to himself. This is duly signed by Mrs. Clemm, and printed over her signature in the published editions of Poe's works. But if the wording of this curious paper be carefully observed, it will be noted that nothing whatever is said in it of any request by Poe that Dr. Griswold should write a memoir of his life. This duty was properly assigned to Mr. Willis — of all men familiar with the subject, the most competent to fulfil such a task, — and his tender and manly tribute to the stricken genius was all that could have been wished, all that the world called for.

Mrs. Clemm had no idea, at the time she signed the paper, which she scarcely understood, that Dr. Griswold had any intention of supplementing Mr. Willis's obituary with any memoir by his own pen. It was a piece of gratuitous malice —

the act of a fiend exulting over a dead and helpless victim.

The tone of Poe's critique of Griswold, in his
review of the "Poets and Poetry of America,"
which unquestionably inspired the reverend doctor's malignant hatred, scathing as it is, will
impress the reader with its outspoken manliness
and integrity of purpose. What a contrast to
the biography that, while undermining the very
foundations of Poe's moral and social character,
yet hypocritically professes · to be dictated by
friendship, and written in a *generous spirit!*
We are convinced that Dr. Griswold's precious
specimen of his generosity will go on record in
the history of literature as an everlasting monument of his despicable meanness.

It is certainly to be regretted that the vindica-
tions of the poet, after his death, were left to the
ephemeral fate of newspaper issue only, and that
no permanent place has, in any American memoir of Poe, been given to the manly and spirited
defence of the poet, written by George R. Graham, and published in "Graham's Magazine" in
1850.

Mr. Graham was peculiarly fitted to speak of

the maligned poet, for no one of Poe's literary contemporaries had known him as intimately, both in the mercantile and the domestic relations.

His testimony to the memory of the stricken genius will, it is to be hoped, be forever embalmed in all future biographies of the poet; for, without it, none would be complete.

We quote it here, as the most important tribute to the poet's personal worth, ever offered by one of his contemporaries.

My Dear Willis, —

In an article of yours which accompanies the two beautiful volumes of the writings of Edgar Allan Poe, you have spoken with so much truth and delicacy of the deceased, and, with the magical touch of genius, have called so warmly up before me the memory of our lost friend as you and I both seem to have known him, that I feel warranted in addressing to you the few plain words I have to say in defence of his character as set down by Mr. Griswold.

Although the article, it seems, appeared originally in the "New York Tribune," it met my eye for the first time in the volumes before me.

I now purpose to take exception to it in the most
public manner. I knew Mr. Poe well, far better
than Mr. Griswold; and by the memory of old
times, when he was an editor of "Graham," I
pronounce this exceedingly ill-timed and unappreciative estimate of the character of our lost
friend, UNFAIR AND UNTRUE. It is Mr. Poe as
seen by the writer while laboring under a fit of
the nightmare, but so dark a picture has no resemblance to the LIVING man. Accompanying
these beautiful volumes, it is an immortal infamy,
the death's head over the entrance to the garden
of beauty, a horror that clings to the brow of
morning, whispering of murder. It haunts the
memory through every page of his writings,
leaving upon the heart a sensation of utter gloom,
a feeling almost of terror. The only relief we
feel is in knowing that it is not true, that it is a
fancy sketch of a perverted, jaundiced vision.
The man who could deliberately say of Edgar
Allan Poe, in a notice of his life and writings
prefacing the volumes which were to become a
priceless souvenir to all who loved him, that his
death might startle many, "BUT THAT FEW WOULD
BE GRIEVED BY IT," and blast the whole fame of

the man by such a paragraph as follows, is a judge dishonored. He is not Mr. Poe's peer, and I challenge him before the country even as a juror in the case :

"His harsh experience had deprived him of all faith in man or woman. He had made up his mind upon the numberless complexities of the social world, and the whole system with him was an imposture. This conviction gave a direction to his shrewd and naturally unamiable character. Still, though he regarded society as COMPOSED ALTOGETHER OF VILLAINS, the sharpness of his intellect was not of that kind which enabled him to cope with villainy, while it continually caused him, by overshots, to fail of the success of honesty. He was in many respects like Francis Vivian in Bulwer's novel of 'The Caxtons.' Passion, in him, comprehended many of the worst emotions which militate against human happiness. You could not contradict him, but you raised quick choler; YOU COULD NOT SPEAK OF WEALTH, BUT HIS CHEEK PALED WITH GNAWING ENVY. The astonishing natural advantages of this poor boy, — his beauty, his readiness, the daring spirit that breathed around him like a fiery atmosphere, had raised his constitutional self-confidence into an arrogance that turned his very claims to admiration into prejudices against him. IRASCIBLE, ENVIOUS, BAD ENOUGH, but not the worst, for these salient angles were all varnished over with a cold, repellant cynicism; his passions vented themselves in sneers. THERE SEEMED TO HIM NO MORAL SUSCEPTIBILITY; and, WHAT WAS MORE REMARKABLE IN A PROUD NATURE, LITTLE OR NOTHING OF THE TRUE POINT OF HONOR. He had, too,

Now this is dastardly, and, what is worse, it
is false. It is very adroitly done, with phrases
very well turned, and with gleams of truth shin-
ing out from a setting so dusky, as to look devil-
ish. Mr. Griswold does not feel the worth of
the man he has undervalued; he had no sympathies in common with him, and has allowed
old prejudices and old enmities to steal, insensi-
bly perhaps, into the coloring of his picture.
They were for years totally uncongenial, if not
enemies, and during that period Mr. Poe, in a
scathing lecture upon "The Poets of America,"
gave Mr. Griswold some raps over the knuckles
of force sufficient to be remembered. He had,
too, in the exercise of his functions as critic, put
to death summarily the literary reputation of
some of Mr. Griswold's best friends; and their
ghosts cried in vain for him to avenge them during Poe's lifetime; and it almost seems as if
the present hacking at the cold remains of him

who struck them down, is a sort of compensation for duty long delayed, for reprisal long desired, but deferred. But without this, the opportunities afforded Mr. Griswold to estimate the character of Poe occurred, in the main, after his stability had been wrecked, his whole nature in a degree changed, and with all his prejudices aroused and active. Nor do I consider Mr. Griswold COMPETENT, with all the opportunities he may have cultivated or acquired, to act as his judge, to dissect that subtle and singularly fine intellect, to probe the motives and weigh the actions of that proud heart. His whole nature, that distinctive presence of the departed, which now stands impalpable, yet in strong outline before me, as I knew him and FELT him to be, eludes the rude grasp of a mind so warped and uncongenial as Mr. Griswold's.

But it may be said, my dear Willis, that Mr. Poe himself deputed him to act as his literary executor, and that he must have felt some confidence, in his ability at least, if not in his integrity, to perform the functions imposed, with discretion and honor. I do not purpose, now, to enter into any examination of the appointment of Mr.

Griswold, nor of the wisdom of his appointment, to the solemn trust of handing the fair
fame of the deceased, unimpaired, to that posterity
to which the dying poet bequeathed his legacy,
but simply to question its faithful performance.
Among the true friends of Poe in this city — and
he had some such here — there are those, I am
sure, that HE did not class among VILLAINS ; nor
do THEY feel easy when they see their old friend
dressed out, in his grave, in the habiliments of a
scoundrel. There is something to them in this
mode of procedure on the part of the literary executor that does not chime in with their notions
of "the true point of honor." They had all of
them looked upon our departed friend as singularly indifferent to wealth for its own sake, but
as very positive in his opinions that the scale of
social merit was not of the highest; that mind,
somehow, was apt to be left out of the estimate
altogether ; and, partaking somewhat of his free
way of thinking, his friends are startled to find
they have entertained very unamiable convic-
tions. As to his "quick choler" when he was
contradicted, it depended a good deal upon the
party denying, as well as upon the subject dis-

cussed. He was quick, it is true, to perceive
mere quacks in literature, and somewhat apt to
be hasty when pestered with them; but upon
most other questions his natural amiability was
not easily disturbed. Upon a subject that he
understood thoroughly, he felt some right to be
positive, if not arrogant, when addressing pre-
tenders. His " astonishing natural advantages "
HAD been very assiduously cultivated; his "daring spirit " was the anointed of genius; his self-
confidence the proud conviction of both; and it
was with something of a lofty scorn that he AT-
TACKED, as well as repelled, a crammed scholar
of the hour, who attempted to palm upon him his
ill-digested learning. Literature with him was
religion; and he, its high priest, with a whip
of scorpions, scourged the money-changers from
the temple. · In all else, he had the docility and
kind-heartedness of a child. No man was more ··
quickly touched by a kindness, none more prompt
to return for an injury. For three or four years
I knew him intimately, and for eighteen months
saw him almost daily, much of the time writing
or conversing at the same desk, knowing all his
hopes, his fears, and little annoyances of life, as

well as his high-hearted struggle with adverse
fate ; yet he was always the same polished gentlemen, the quiet, unobtrusive, thoughtful scholar,
the devoted husband, frugal in his personal expenses, punctual and unwearied in his industry,
AND THE SOUL OF HONOR in all his transactions.
This, of course, was in his better days, and by
them WE judge the man. But even after his
habits had changed, there was no literary man to
whom I would more readily advance money for
labor to be done. He kept his accounts, small
as they were, with the accuracy of a banker. I
append an account sent to me in his own hand,
long after he had left Philadelphia, and after all
knowledge of the transactions it recited had escaped my memory. I had returned him the story
of "The Gold Bug," at his own request, as he
found that he could dispose of it very advanta-
geously elsewhere : —

We were square when I sold you the "Versification"
  article, for which you gave me, first, $25, and after-
    wards $7 — in all $32 00
Then you bought "The Gold Bug" for . . . 52 00
I got both these back, so that I owed . . . $84 00
You lent Mrs. Clemm 12 50
Making in all $96 50

The review of " Flaccus " was 3 3-4 pp.,
which, at $4, is $15 00
Lowell's poem is 10 00
The review of Channing, 4 pp., is $16, of
which I got $6, leaving , . . 10 00
The review of Halleck, 4 pp., is $16, of
which I got $10, leaving . . . 6 00
The review of Reynolds, 2 pp. . . 8 00
The review of Longfellow, 5 pp., is $20,
of which I got $10, leaving . . . 10 00
So that I have paid in all . . . 59 00

Which leaves still due by me $37 50

This, I find, was his uniform habit with others
as well as myself, carefully recalling to mind his
indebtedness with the fresh article sent. And
this is the man who had " no moral susceptibility," and little or nothing of the " true point of
honor." It may be a very plain business view of
the question, but it strikes his friends that it may
pass as something, as times go.

I shall never forget how solicitous of the happiness of his wife and mother-in-law he was
whilst one of the editors of " GRAHAM'S MAGA-
ZINE ;" his whole efforts seemed to be to procure
the comfort and welfare of his home. Except
for their happiness, and the natural ambition of

having a magazine of his own, I never heard him
deplore the want of wealth. The truth is, he
cared little for money, and knew less of its value,
for he seemed to have no personal expenses.
What he received from me, in regular monthly
instalments, went directly into the hands of his
mother-in-law for family comforts, and TWICE
only I remember his purchasing some rather ex-
pensive luxuries for his house, and then he was
nervous to the degree of misery until he had, by
extra articles, covered what he considered an im-
prudent indebtedness. His love for his wife was
a sort of rapturous worship of the spirit of beauty
which he felt was fading before his eyes. I have
seen him hovering around her when she was ill,
with all the fond fear and tender anxiety of a
mother for her first-born, her slightest cough caus-
ing in him a shudder, a heart-chill that was visible.
I rode out, one summer evening, with them, and
the remembrance of his watchful eyes eagerly bent
upon the slightest change of hue in that loved
face haunts me yet as the memory of a sad strain.
It was the hourly ANTICIPATION of her loss that
made him a sad and thoughtful man, and lent a
mournful melody to his undying song.

It is true, that later in life Poe had much of
those morbid feelings which a life of poverty and
d'sappointment is so apt to engender in the heart
of man—the sense of having been ill-used, mis-
understood, and put aside by men of far less
ability, and of none,—which preys upon the heart
and clouds the brain of many a child of song.
A consciousness of the inequalities of life, and of
the abundant power of mere wealth, allied even
to vulgarity, to override all distinctions, and to
thrust itself, bedaubed with dirt and glittering
with tinsel, into the high places of society, and
the chief seats of the synagogue; whilst he, a
worshipper of the beautiful and true, who listened
to the voices of angels and held delighted companionship with them as the cold throng swept
disdaindfully by him, was often in danger of
being thrust out, houseless, homeless, beggared,
upon the world, with all his fine feelings strung
to a tension of agony when he thought of his
beautiful and delicate wife, dying hourly before
his eyes.   What wonder that he then poured out
the vials of a long-treasured bitterness upon the
injustice and hollowness of all society around
him.

The very natural question "Why did he not work and thrive?" is easily answered. It will not be ASKED by the many who know the precarious tenure by which literary men hold a mere living in this country. The avenues through which they can profitably reach the country are few, and crowded with aspirants for bread, as well as fame. The unfortunate tendency to cheapen every literary work to the lowest point of beggarly flimsiness in price and profit, prevents even the well-disposed from extending anything like an adequate support to even a part of the great throng which genius, talent, education, and even misfortune, force into the struggle. The character of Poe's mind was of such an order as not to be very widely in demand. The class of educated mind which he could readily and profitably address was small—the channels through which he could do so at all were few—and publishers all, or nearly all, contented with such pens as were already engaged, hesitated to incur the expense of his to an extent which would sufficiently remunerate him; hence, when he was fairly at sea, connected permanently with no publication, he suffered all the horrors of prospective destitution, with scarcely the ability of providing for immediate necessities; and at such moments, alas! the tempter often came, and as as you have truly said, "ONE GLASS" of wine made him a madman. Let the moralist, who stands upon "tufted carpet," and surveys his smoking board, the fruits of his individual toil or mercantile adventure, pause before he let the anathema, trembling upon his lips, fall upon a man like Poe, who, wandering from publisher to publisher, with his fine, print-like manuscript, scrupulously clean and neatly rolled, finds no market for his brain—with despair at heart, misery ahead, for himself and his loved ones, and gaunt famine dogging at his heels, thus sinks by the wayside, before the demon that watches his steps and whispers OBLIVION. Of all the miseries which God, or his own vices, inflict upon man, none are so terrible as that of having the strong and willing arm struck down to a childlike inefficiency, while the Heart and the Will have the purpose of a giant's out-doing We must remember, too, that the very organization of such a mind as that of Poe—the very tension and tone of his exquisitely strung nerves—

the passionate yearnings of his soul for the beautiful and true, utterly unfitted him for the rude jostlings and fierce competitorship of trade. The only drafts of his that could be honored were those upon his brain. The unpeopled air — the caverns of ocean — the decay and mystery that hang around old castles — the thunder of wind through the forest aisles — the spirits that rode the blast, by all but him unseen — and the deep, metaphysical creations which floated through the chambers of his soul — were his only wealth, the High Change where only his signature was valid for rubies.

Could he have stepped down and chronicled small beer, made himself the shifting toady of the hour, and, with bow and cringe, hung upon the steps of greatness, sounding the glory of third-rate ability with a penny trumpet, he would heve been fêted alive, and PERHAPS been praised when dead. But, no! his views of the duty of the critic were stern, and he felt that in praising an unworthy writer he committed dishonor. His pen was regulated by the highest sense of DUTY. By a keen analysis he separated and studied each piece which the skilful mechanist had put together. No part, however insignificant or apparently unimportant, escaped the rigid and patient scrutiny of his sagacious mind. The unfitted joint proved the bungler — the slightest blemish was a palpable fraud. He was the scrutinizing lapidary, who detected and exposed the most minute flaw in diamonds. The gem of first water shone the brighter for the truthful setting of his calm praise. He had the finest touch of soul for beauty — a delicate and hearty appreciation of worth. If his praise appeared tardy, it was of priceless value when given. It was true as well as sincere. It was the stroke of honor that at once knighted the receiver. It was in the world of MIND that he was king; and, with a fierce audacity, he felt and proclaimed himself autocrat. As critic, he was despotic, supreme. Yet no man with more readiness would soften a harsh expression at the request of a friend, or if he himself felt that he had infused too great a degree of bitterness into his article, none would more readily soften it down after it was in type — though still maintaining the justness of his critical views. I do not believe that he wrote to give pain; but in combating what he conceived to be error, he used the strongest word that presented itself, even in conversation. He labored not so much to reform as to EXTERMINATE error, and thought the shortest process was to pull it up by the roots.

He was a worshipper of INTELLECT—longing to grasp the power of mind that moves the stars—to bathe his soul in the dreams of seraphs. He was himself all ethereal, of a fine essence, that moved in an atmosphere of spirits —of spiritual beauty, overflowing and radiant— twin-brother with the angels, feeling their flashing wings upon his heart, and almost clasping them in his embrace. Of them, and as an expectant archangel of that high order of intellect, stepping out of himself, as it were, and interpreting the time he revelled in delicious luxury in a world beyond, with an audacity which we fear in madmen, but in genius worship as the inspiration of heaven.

But my object, in throwing together a few thoughts upon the character of Edgar Allan Poe, was not to attempt an elaborate criticism, but to say what might palliate grave faults that have been attributed to him, and to meet by facts un-

just accusation; in a word, to give a mere outline of the man as he lived before me.   I think I
am warranted in saying to Mr. Griswold that he
must review his decision.   It will not stand the
calm scrutiny of his own judgment, or of time,
while it must be regarded by all the friends of
Mr. Poe as an ill-judged and misplaced calumny
upon that gifted son of genius.

Yours truly,
Geo. R. Graham.

Philadelphia, February 2, 1850.

To N. P. Willis, Esq.

Numerous other memoirs and biographies of
Poe have also appeared since his death.   Many
of them have been founded upon Griswold's, and
have already been alluded to.   Such should be
dismissed without other consideration than that
they have unquestionably had, aside from the
unjust estimate which they have conveyed of the
poet, a deteriorating effect upon the popularity
of his works, both in America and England.
The effect of the Griswold biography upon the
intelligent reader may be exactly measured by
the impression formed by an English reviewer of

Hannay's biography, founded upon Griswold's; to wit, —

" Should any man of taste and sense, not acquainted with Poe, be so unfortunate as to look at Dr. Griswold's preface before reading the poetry, it is extremely probable he will throw the book into the fire, in indignation at the self-conceit and affected smartness by which the preface is characterized."

In 1859, Mrs. S. H. Whitman, in her volume " Edgar Poe and his Critics," which we have had occasion to repeatedly commend in this volume, made a most valuable contribution to literary biography, and offered a significant tribute to the memory of Poe, which was probably not fully appreciated, issued, as it was, at a time when the country was disturbed and unsettled by the excitements of the impending civil war.

Mr. James Woods Davidson made a very complete collection of Poe material, which was, unfortunately, destroyed during the seige of Charleston.

Mr. Thomas Cottrell Clarke made a collection which he eventually disposed of, and to which we have had access in the preparation of this work.

It is not to be regretted that Mr. Clarke never completed and published his memoir, for although a near personal friend of the poet, he was lacking in the enterprise and determination necessary to the adequate fulfilment of such a task.

Mr. J. H. Ingram, of London, possessing both enterprise and determination, has written and published a memoir of Poe, which, considering the disadvantage of collecting literary material at the distance of three thousand miles from the poet's birthplace, is a creditable work, although, in some essential points, it is unreliable.

Mr. R. H. Stoddard wrote an interesting memoir for Routledge's London edition of the poet's works.

Mr. Thomas C. Latto, now of Brooklyn, New York, has made a collection, designing, it is understood, to write a memoir of the poet.

Francis Gerry Fairfield wrote a paper, entitled "A Mad Man of Letters," for "Scribner's Magazine," October, 1875, in which he presumed to class the author of "The Raven" as an epileptic. The article was written, like many others concerning Poe, with a reckless disregard of facts, and was unanswerably controverted by Mrs. S. H.

Whitman, in a letter published in "The New York Tribune."

Mr. Eugene Didier, of Baltimore, has written a biographical sketch of the poet, to preface a new edition of Poe, issued by W. J. Widdleton, of New York.

Miss Sarah E. Rice, of Baltimore, aided by Wm. Hand Browne, Esq., of that city, has prepared a memorial volume, containing an account of the monument erected in Baltimore to the memory of the poet, and some interesting reminiscences of Poe by one of his schoolmates.

The late J. P. Thompson wrote a lecture on Poe, which was, we are informed, delivered in Baltimore. These, with our lecture, "The Romance of Edgar A. Poe," our vindication of the poet originally published in "Lotos Leaves," and subsequently in the Diamond edition of Poe's poems, issued by Widdleton, and our reminiscences of the poet in "Laurel Leaves," comprise the principal isolated papers on Poe, *not* founded on Griswold, that have been published, aside from the sketches to be found in the cyclopædias, and the numerous contributions that have, from time to time, appeared in the newspapers.

Before alluding to the most significant public tribute ever offered to the memory of Poe, the erection of the monument dedicated at Baltimore in November, 1875, it should be stated that the impression that no fitting marks of respect to the dead poet, have ever been offered by his relatives, is erroneous. A suitable slab, bearing the inscription, "*Hic tandem felice conduntur Reliquiae*, Edgar Allan Poe," was prepared by the order of Neilson Poe, Esq.

But the relentless fate that pursued the unhappy poet during his lifetime, followed him after death, and a phenomenal catastrophe prevented the erection of the slab over his grave.

On the day before it was to have been erected, a freight train on the Northern Central Railroad jumped the track, and ran into the marble yard, near by the depot, in which the slab was placed, awaiting transportation to the cemetery. The slab was directly in the course of the heavy train, and was shivered to atoms.

Poe's grave, therefore, remained neglected until efforts of the Baltimore School Teachers Association, and the munificence of George W. Childs, Esq., of Philadelphia, secured the substantial monument now placed over his tomb. The interesting ceremonies of the dedication took place November 17, 1875. The account here given is gathered from the graphic description published in "The Cincinnati Commercial," and from the Baltimore papers of November 18.

"For several years, the school teachers of this city have been accumulating a fund for the purpose of erecting a suitable memorial above the last resting-place of this rare genius, and they were generously aided in their efforts by Geo. W. Childs, of Philadelphia, whose donation amounted to nearly half the cost of the monument. The ceremonies of unveiling this memorial to-day were most interesting. Crowds were assembled at the western female high school, adjoining Westminster Church, where, ten years ago, the first entertainment on behalf of the movement was given.

"Professor Elliott gave a history of the movement, while Professor Shepherd's scholarly production treated more exclusively of 'Poe as a poet and man of genius.'

"The reminiscences of Mr. Latrobe were delivered in a most impressive manner, and were received with the greatest enthusiasm.

"Miss Rice, who has always been most active in the work, read letters from our own poets who were unable to attend, and also one from Alfred Tennyson; and Mr. W. F. Gill, of Boston, who has done much, by his earnest vindication of the poet's memory, to remove false impressions, gave the finest rendition of 'The Raven' to which we ever listened. The large audience was absolutely spell-bound by his perfect elocution; and his resemblance to the recognized ideals of Mr. Poe himself, made the personation of his horror and despair almost painful.

"A few words by Mr. Neilson Poe, cousin of the poet, who was present at his burial, twenty-six years ago, expressing gratification at the completion of the work undertaken by the committee, concluded the exercises in the hall.

"While the monument was being unveiled, a dirge was sung, and a superb wreath of laurel and choice flowers, the contribution of the dramatic profession, of which Poe's mother was a member, was placed upon it; after which "Annabel Lee" was recited in the same masterly manner by Mr. Gill, and a lady gave a very good rendition of 'The Bells.'

"The monument is a plain Grecian obelisk of purest marble upon a granite base, and at present is only ornamented with a medallion bust of the poet, with his name and the dates of his birth and death. An inscription written by Tennyson is to be added hereafter.

"The day was lovely, though rather windy and cold, and, to-night, the pale beams of the moon will shine on the grave — no longer neglected — of Edgar Allan Poe."

The platform at the head of the hall was filled with a number of gentlemen. Principals of the high schools, those who were to take part in the exercises, gentlemen who had been acquaintances or associates of the poetic genius in honor of whose memory the meeting was held, and other invited guests. Among them was prominent the venerable head of Walt Whitman, the poet, his silver hair sweeping his shoulders; Prof. John Hewitt, once editor of the "Saturday Visitor," in which Poe's weird story of "The Manuscript Found in a Bottle" first appeared; Dr. John H. Snodgrass, also a former editor of the "Visitor," Prof. N. C. Brooks, who edited the "American Magazine," in which some of Poe's earliest

productions appeared, and Prof. Joseph Clarke, a
very venerable gentleman, whose school at Richmond, Virginia, had been attended by Poe when
a boy, were also upon the platform.   Among
others were Prof. J. C. Kinear, of Pembroke
Academy ; Dr. N. H. Morison, provost of Pea-
body Institute ; John T. Morris, Esq., president
of the School Board; the Rev. Dr. Julius E.
Grammer, Judge Garey, Joseph Merrefield, Esq.,
Dr. John G. Morris, Neilson Poe, Esq., Ichabod
Jean, Esq., Summerfield Baldwin, Joseph J.
Stewart, Esq., Professors Thayer and Hollings-
head, John T. Ford, Esq., George Small, Esq.,
the Faculty of the Baltimore City College, M. A.
Newell, Esq., State School Superintendent, as
well as those who were to take part in the proceedings.   The exercises began shortly after two
o'clock with the performance of the "Pilgrims'
Chorus" of Verdi, by the Philharmonic Society,
who occupied raised seats in the rear of the hall,
under the direction of Professor Remington Fair-
lamb.

At the close of the music, Professor William
Elliott, Jr., president of the Baltimore City College, delivered the following address, containing the

HISTORY OF THE MOVEMENT.

"LADIES AND GENTLEMEN,—I purpose, in discharging the duty assigned me on this occasion, to give a brief historical shetch of the movement which culminates, to-day, in the dedication of a monument to the memory of the great American poet, Edgar Allan Poe, the first and only memorial expression of the kind ever given to an American on account of literary excellence.

"This extraordinary and unique genius, born in Boston, January 20, 1809, during a brief sojourn of his parents in that place, died on the 7th of October, 1849, in this city, which is undoubtedly entitled to claim him as one of her distinguished sons. Two days thereafter, on the 9th of October, his mortal remains were interred in the cemetery attached to the Westminster Presbyterian Church, adjoining the building in which we are now assembled.

"In this connection, acting as a truthful chronicler, I deem it proper to state some facts in relation to the circumstances of the interment. The reliability of the statement I shall now make is sufficiently attested by the evidence of at least three of the gentlemen present on that occasion —possibly the only three who yet survive.

. " I have been informed that the day was, for the
season, more than ordinarily unpleasant, the weather being raw and cold ; indeed, just such a day
as it would have been more comfortable to spend
within than without doors.

"The time of the interment was about four
o'clock in the afternoon ; the attendance of persons at the grave, possibly a consequence of the
state of the weather, was limited to eight, certainly to not more than nine, persons, one of
these being a lady.

"Of the number known to have been present
were, Hon. Z. Collins Lee, a classmate of the
deceased at the University of Virginia ; Henry
Herring, Esq., a connection of Mr. Poe ; Rev.
W. T. D. Clemm, a relative of Mr. Poe's wife ;
our well-known fellow-citizen, Neilson Poe, Esq.,
a cousin of the poet ; Edmund Smith, Esq., and
wife, the latter being a first cousin of Poe, and
at this time his nearest living relative in this city,
and possibly Dr. Snodgrass, the editor of the
"Saturday Visitor," the paper in which the prize
story written by Poe first made its appearance.
The clergyman who officiated at the grave was
Rev. W. T. D. Clemm, already mentioned, a

member of the Baltimore Conference of the Methodist Episcopal Church, who read the impressive burial service used by that denomination of Christians, after which, all that was mortal of Edgar Allan Poe was gently committed to its mother earth.

"Another item, which it may not be inappropriate to record in this historical compend, I will now mention, namely, that George W. Spence, who officiated as sexton at the burial of Mr. Poe, is the same person who, after the lapse of twenty-six years, has superintended the removal of his remains, and those of his loving and beloved mother-in-law, Mrs. Clemm, and their re-interment in the lot in which the monument now stands.

"For a number of years after the burial of the poet, no steps seem to have been taken toward making his grave, until, at length, a stone was prepared for this purpose by order of Neilson Poe, Esq. Unfortunately, however, this stone never served the purpose for which it was designed. A train of cars accidentally ran into the establishment of Mr. Hugh Sisson, at which place the stone was at the time, and so damaged it as to render it unfit to be used as intended.

" Another series of years intervened, but yet no movement to mark the grave. True, articles almost innumerable, *ad nauseam*, made their appearance at short intervals during that time in different newspapers, but the authors of those articles were mostly of that class of persons who employ their energies in finding fault with others, totally oblivious of the fact that they themselves, no less, deserved the censure they so liberally meted out to others.

" 'Poe's neglected grave' was the stereotyped expression of these modern Jeremiahs. Nor were they content to indulge in lamentations; not unfrequently our good city was soundly berated because of its alleged want of appreciation of the memory of one whose ashes, they intimated, had he been an Englishman, instead of filling an unmarked grave in an obscure cemetery, would have had accorded to them a place in that grand old abbey which England has appropriated as a mausoleum for her distinguished dead.

" But the 'neglected grave' was not always to remain such. At a regular meeting of the Public School Teachers' Association, held in this hall, October 7, 1865, Mr. John Basil, Jr., principal of

No. 8 Grammar School, offered a paper, of which
the following is a copy : —

"'Whereas it has been represented to certain members of
the Association that the mortal remains of Edgar Allan Poe,
are interred in the cemetery of the Westminster Church. without even so much as a stone to mark the spot; therefore,
"'Resolved that a committee of five be appointed by the
president of this Association to devise some means best
adapted, in their judgment, to perpetuate the memory of one
who has contributed so largely to American literature.'

"This resolution was unanimously adopted, and
a committee, consisting of Messrs. Basil, Baird
and J. J. G. Webster, Miss Veeder and Miss
Wise, appointed to carry out the purpose named.

"This committee reported in favor of the erection of a monument, and recommended that
measures be at once taken to secure the funds
necessary to accomplish this object.   This rec-
ommendation was heartily indorsed by the Association, and, without delay, the committee entered
upon the work of raising the funds.

"In this work the young ladies of the western
female high school took an active and, as will
be seen, a successful part.   An entertainment of
select readings by the pupils of that school, held

in this hall, on the evening of October 10, 1865, under the superintendence of Miss S. S. Rice, yielded the handsome sum of $380. A literary and musical entertainment, held in Concordia Hall, December 7, 1865, in which the pupils of the eastern and western female high schools and those of Baltimore City College took part, increased the fund by the addition thereto of $75.92. May 15, 1866, a contribution of $50 was received from Prof. Charles Davies, of New York, and on the 19th of the same month a donation of $54 was received as an offering of the young ladies of 'Troy Female Seminary.' These sums, with interest added, amounted, as per report of Thomas D. Baird, treasurer, submitted March 23, 1871, to $587.02. The enthusiasm that characterized the undertaking at the outset seemed now to have greatly abated, and serious thoughts were consequently entertained of abandoning the project. At this juncture, a new committee, consisting of Messrs. Elliott, Kerr and Hamilton, Miss Rice and Miss Baer, was appointed to consider the matter.

"After mature deliberation this committee reported, April 15, 1872, as follows: "First, resolved, that the money now in the hands of the treasurer of the 'Poe Memorial Fund,' be appropriated to the erection of a monument, the same to be placed over Poe's remains. Second, that a committee of five be appointed by the president, with power to act as stated in the first resolution." These resolutions were adopted, and the committee therein provided for, appointed as follows : Wm. Elliott, Jr., A. S. Kerr, Alexander Hamilton, Miss S. S. Rice and Miss E. A. Baer. September 2, 1874, this committee received, from the estate of Dr. Thomas D. Baird, deceased, the late treasurer of the 'Poe Memorial Fund,' $627.55, the amount of principal and interest to that date, which was immediately deposited in the Chesapeake Bank, of this city. Believing that this amount could be increased to $1000 by donations from some of our fellow-citizens who favored the project, the committee applied to Mr. George A. Frederick, architect of the City Hall, for the design of a monument to cost about that sum.

"Mr. Frederick, in due time, submitted a design 'at once simple, chaste and dignified,' but requiring for its realization much more than the amount included in the expectations of the committee. Moreover, a new feature was now introduced, that of placing a medallion likeness of the poet on one of the panels of the monument, which would still further increase the cost. With a view of determining whether the amount necessary to complete the monument, according to the proportions it had now assumed, could be raised, applications were made to a number of our citizens for contributions. From one, of acknowledged æsthetic taste, a check of $100 was promptly received. Two other gentlemen contributed $50 each, while Miss S. S. Rice, a member of the committee, collected in small sums $52 more.

"A knowledge of the 'world-wide' known liberality of Mr. George W. Childs, of Philadelphia, formerly one of our fellow townsmen, induced the chairman of the committee to drop him a note on the subject. Within twenty-four hours, a reply was received from that gentleman, expressive of his willingness to make up the estimated deficiency of $650.

"The necessary amount having now been secured, the committee proceeded to place the construction and erection of the monument in the hands of Mr. Hugh Sisson, his proposal being the most liberal one received. How faithfully he has executed his commission will be seen when the covering that now veils the monument is removed. No one, so well as the chairman of the committee, knows how anxious Mr. Sisson has been to meet even more than the expectations of those most concerned. To his generous liberality are we largely indebted for the reproduction of the classic lineaments of the poet, in the beautiful and highly artistic medallion that adds so much to the attractiveness of the monument.

"To most of those present, I presume, it is known that the lot in which the monument is now located is not the one in which it was first placed. In deference to what was considered by the committee the popular wish, the monument was removed from its first location to its present one. The remains of Mr. Poe, and also those of his mother-in-law, were, as before intimated, removed at the same time. The new lot was secured mainly through the efforts of Mr. John T. Morris, president of the school board, to whom, and to all others who have in any way contributed to the consummation of this undertaking, I wish here, on behalf of the committee, to render thanks.

"In conclusion, allow me to congratulate all concerned that Poe's grave is no longer a neglected one."

Upon the conclusion of Professor Elliott's address, which was listened to with deep attention, Miss Sarah S. Rice was introduced to the audience. To this lady, well known to the public from her elocutionary attainments, the greatest possible credit is due for the successful completion of the enterprise. The first money raised for the erection of the monument was through her personal efforts, and the entire monument, from its inception to the close, has enjoyed the benefits of her unremitting attention and effort. Miss Rice read the following

LETTERS FROM THE POETS,
In response to Invitations to be present on the Occasion.

FROM MR. BRYANT.

CUMMINGTON, Mass., September 18, 1875.

Dear Madam, — I return my thanks for the obliging invitation contained in your letter of the 14th, and for the kind words with which it is accompanied. For various reasons, however, among which is my advanced age, it is not in my power to be present at the ceremonies of which you speak, and I have only to make my best acknowledgment to those who have done me the honor to think of me in connection with them. I am, madam, truly yours,

Wm. C. Bryant.

Miss S. S. Rice.

FROM MR. LOWELL.

Cambridge, 18th October, 1875.

Dear Madam, — I regret very much that it will be quite impossible for me to be present at the very interesting ceremony of unveiling the monument to Poe. I need not assure you that I sympathize very heartily with the sentiment which led to its erection.

I remain very truly yours,

J. R. Lowell.

Miss Sarah S. Rice, Cor. Sec. of the
Poe Monument Association, Baltimore.

FROM MRS. WHITMAN.

Providence, R.I., November 5, 1875.

Miss Sarah S. Rice.

My dear Madam, — Your most kind and gratifying letter, conveying to me an invitation to be present at the unveiling of the monument to the memory of our great American poet, was duly received. I need not say to you that the generous efforts of the association in whose behalf you write have called forth my warmest sympathy and most grateful appreciation. The work was long delayed, and has been consummated at the right time, and through the most congenial and appropriate agencies.

I am, most sincerely and most gratefully, yours,

SARAH HELEN WHITMAN.

FROM MR. WHITTIER.

AMESBURY, 9th mo., 21, 1875.

To SARAH S. RICE.

Dear friend, — The extraordinary genius of Edgar A. Poe is now acknowledged the world over, and the proposed tribute to his memory indicates a full appreciation of his own intellectual gifts on the part of the city of his birth. As a matter of principle, I do not favor ostentatious monuments for the dead, but sometimes it seems the only way to express the appreciation which circumstances, in some measure, may have denied to the living man.

I am not able to be present at the inauguration of the monument. Pray express my thanks to the ladies and gentlemen for whom thy letter speaks, for the invitation. Acknowledging the kind terms in which that invitation was conveyed on thy part, I am very truly thy friend,

JOHN G. WHITTIER.

FROM DR. HOLMES.

BOSTON, September 18, 1875.

Dear Miss Rice, — In answer to your kind invitation, I regret that I cannot say that I hope to be present at the ceremony of placing a monument over the grave of your poet. Your city has already honored valor and patriotism by the erection of stately columns. Republics are said to be ungrateful, perhaps because they have short memories, forgetting wrongs as quickly as benefits. But your city has shown that it can remember, and has taught us all the lesson of gratitude. No one, surely, needs a mausoleum less than the poet.

> His monument shall be his gentle verse,
> Which eyes not yet created shall o'erread;
> And tongues to be, his being shall rehearse
> When all the breathers of this world are dead.

Yet we would not leave him without a stone to mark the spot where the hands that " waked to ecstacy the living lyre " were laid in the dust. He that can confer an immortality which will outlast bronze and granite deserves this poor tribute, not for his sake so much as ours. The hearts of all who reverence the inspiration of genius, who can look tenderly upon the infirmities too often attending it, who can feel for its misfortunes, will sympathize with you as you gather around the resting place of all that was mortal of Edgar Allan Poe, and raise the stone inscribed with one of the few names which will outlive the graven record meant to perpetuate its remembrance.

Believe me very truly yours,

O. W. HOLMES.

FROM MR. ALDRICH.

BOSTON, Mass., October 10, 1875.

SARAH S. RICE, Cor. Sec.

Dear Madam, —I hasten to acknowledge the receipt of your letter inviting me to attend the inaugural ceremonies of the monument to Edgar Allan Poe. It is with the deepest regret that I find myself unable to accept the invitation. I have just returned from a long absence abroad, and my private affairs demand my closest attention. The duties and engagements which I have been obliged to put aside during the past six or seven months leave me no time to write anything that would serve your purpose. But for this, I would come in person to lay my tribute, with the other more worthy offerings, on Poe's grave. Your desire to honor his genius is in the heart of every man of letters, though perhaps no American author stands so little in need of a monument to perpetuate his memory as the author of "The Raven." His imperishable fame is in all lands.

With thanks for your courtesy, I remain,

> Very truly yours,
> THOMAS BAILEY ALDRICH.

FROM MRS. PRESTON.

LEXINGTON, Virginia, October 8.

MISS SARAH S. RICE.

Dear Madam, — Your note and request, so complimentary to myself, has been received.

I thank you for the good opinion which led you to propose the writing of a poem on my part for the prospective inauguration of the Poe Memorial. While it is not in my power to comply with the flattering request, or to be present at the ceremonial, I tender to the committee my thanks, nevertheless, for the honor thus conferred on me.

There would seem to be a slight appropriateness in the proposal made to me, inasmuch as my husband (Colonel Preston, of the Virginia Military College) was a boyish friend of Poe's when they went to school together in Richmond: who used to sit on the same bench with him, and together pore over the same pages of "Horace." To him, as his earliest literary critic — a boy of fourteen — Poe was accustomed to bring his first verses. Even then, youth as he was, he was distinguished by many of the characteristics which marked his after-life.

With every good wish for the entire success of your memorial services, and with renewed thanks to your committee for this mark of regard, believe me, my dear madam, sincerely yours,

MARGARET J. PRESTON.

FROM MR. SAXE.

BROOKLYN, N.Y., October 10, 1875.

To SARAH S. RICE, Professor of Elocution, Baltimore, Maryland: — Of all my letters received during a long confinement by sickness, yours of the 5th instant is the first I have attempted to answer. I employ the hand of another (for I am not yet able to write) to thank you for the kind invitation you send me to assist at the Poe Monument ceremonies, on the 15th instant.

As I cannot hope to be present on that occasion, I avail myself of your friendly note to express my interest in the event, and my admiration of the noble-hearted men and women of Baltimore, who, by the creation of a beautiful and appropriate monument to the memory of Edgar A. Poe, perform a patriotic office which was primarily and peculiarly the duty, as it should have been the pride, of the American *literati*, toward one whose original genius has done so much to adorn and distinguish American literature.

Yours very truly,
JOHN GODFREY SAXE.

Prof. Elliot read the following letter from G. W. Childs, of Philadelphia, regretting that he could not be present : —

PHILADELPHIA, November 15, 1875.

It would be very agreeable to my regard for the memory of Edgar A. Poe to accept your invitation to be present at the dedicatory ceremonies of the Poe Monument, on the 17th inst., but it is quite improbable that I can be with you on that occasion. There is a mournful satisfaction, even in this late tribute to one whose rare genius and sensitive nature were accompanied by so many unhappy experiences of life. Poor Poe! His working-day world was more than full of sorrows, and he seems to have been happy only in his visions outside of real life, or in his dream of a world beyond that in which we all live.

What is now being done by the affectionate friends, and by those who feel that injustice has been done to his memory, may prove to be the starting point of a changed and juster view of his life and character. Although it is far too late to be of service to him, it is not too late to be of benefit to ourselves and others. Those of us who may have felt disposed to censure him, can read with profit the following lines from his " Tamerlane," and especially the last couplet : —

> " I firmly do believe —
> I know — for Death, who comes for me
> From regions of the blest afar,
> Where there is nothing to deceive,
> Hath left his iron gate ajar,
> And rays of truth you cannot see
> Are flashing through eternity."

Yours respectfully,

GEORGE W. CHILDS.

JOSIAH GILBERT HOLLAND.

NEW YORK, Oct. 11, 1875.

Dear Madam — On the 15th of this month I am to be in Wilmington, Ohio, for a lecture; and on the eve of a long Western trip I find myself so crowded with important duties that I cannot even write the letter I have in my heart. I am very glad the genius of Poe is to be formally recognized by ceremony and monument, as it has been long appreciated by untold thousands of people wherever the English language is spoken. I am sorry I cannot be present at the inaugural ceremonies; but you will not miss me. I shall only miss you, and the loyal throng who will gather to bring the dead poet their honors. Thanking you kindly for your invitation,

I am yours truly,

J. G. HOLLAND.

ALFRED TENNYSON.

FARINGFORD, Freshwater, Isle of Wight, Jan. 12, 1875.

I have long been acquainted with Poe's works and am an admirer of them. I am obliged to you for your expressions about myself, and your promise of sending me the design for the poet's monument, and beg you to believe me,

Yours very truly,

A. TENNYSON.

HENRY WADSWORTH LONGFELLOW.

CAMBRIDGE, August 20, 1875.

Dear Madam, — The only lines of Mr. Poe that I now recall as in any way appropriate to the purpose you mention are from a poem entitled " For Annie." They are, —

" The fever called living
Is conquered at last."

But I dare say you will be able to find something better.
In great haste,   Yours truly,

                       HENRY W. LONGFELLOW.

FROM A PERSONAL FRIEND.

BROOKLYN, N.Y., October 11, 1875.

My Dear Miss Rice, — My friend John G. Saxe, to whom
you wrote in regard to the " Poe Monument Association," is
quite unwell; indeed, is confined to his room, and fears he
will not be able to answer your kind request. If, however,
he shall be able, he will at least write you. In the mean time,
at his suggestion, allow me, a personal friend and warm admirer of both the genius and personal worth of our lamented
friend, to say to you and to the association a few words.

I have resided and practised my profession of the law in
Brooklyn for about thirty years. Shortly after I moved here,
in 1845, Mr. Poe and I became personal friends. His last
residence, and where I visited him oftenest, was in a beautiful
secluded cottage at Fordham, fourteen miles above New York.
It was there I often saw his dear wife during her last illness,
and attended her funeral. It was from there that he and his
" dear Muddie " (Mrs. Clemm) often visited me at my house,
frequently, at my urgent solicitation, remaining many days.
When he finally departed on his last trip South, the kissing
and hand-shaking were at my front door. He was hopeful;
we were sad, and tears gushed in torrents as he kissed his
" dear Muddie " and my wife " good-bye." Alas! it proved,
as Mrs. Clemm feared, a final adieu.

A few months afterwards, on receipt of the sad news of his
death, I offered Mrs. C. a home in my family, where she resided till 1858, when she removed to Baltimore to lay her
ashes by the side of her darling Eddie. I hold many of her

precious, loving, grateful letters to me from there, up to a few days before her death.

And now, as to Mr. Poe, he was one of the most affection-ate, kind-hearted men I ever knew. I never witnessed so much tender affection and devoted love as existed in that family of three persons.

His dear Virginia, after her death, was his "Lost Lenore." I have spent weeks in the closest intimacy with Mr. Poe, and I never saw him drink a drop of liquor, wine or beer, in my life, and never saw him under the slightest influence of any stimulants whatever. He was, in truth, a most abstemious and exemplary man. But I learned from Mrs. Clemm that if, on the importunity of a convivial friend, he took a single glass, even wine, it suddenly flashed through his nervous system and excitable brain, and that he was no longer him-self, or responsible for his acts. His biographers have not done his virtues or his genius justice; and to produce a start-ling effect, by contrast, have magnified his errors and attrib-uted to him faults which he never had. He was always, in my presence, the polished gentleman, the profound scholar, the true critic, and the inspired oracular poet; dreaming and spiritual; lofty but sad. His memory is green and fresh in many admiring and loving hearts, and your work of erecting a monument over his grave, if it adds nothing to his fame, reflects honor on you and your association, and upon all who sympathize or assist in your noble work.

I am proud to assure you, and the association through you, that his many friends are grateful and thank you.

> " What recks he of their plaudits now?
> He never deemed them worth his care,
> And death has twined around his brow
> The wreath he was too proud to wear."

Yours truly,   S. D. LEWIS.

FROM A. C. SWINBURNE.

(*From the N. Y. Tribune, Nov.* 27, 1872.)

The following letter from the poet Swinburne — addressed to Miss Sarah S. Rice, the director of the Poe Memorial Committee — was received in Baltimore too late to be read at the dedication of the monument. It indicates the sympathy of genius with genius; and it affords another illustration of the high estimate that English critical thought has placed upon the writings of Poe : —

HOLMWOOD, SHIPLAKE, }
HENLEY-ON-THAMES, Nov. 9, 1875. }

SARAH S. RICE.

Dear Madam, — I have heard, with much pleasure, of the memorial at length raised to your illustrious fellow-citizen.

The genius of Edgar Poe has won, on this side of the Atlantic, such wide and warm recognition that the sympathy, which I cannot hope fitly or fully to express in adequate words, is undoubtedly shared at this moment by hundreds, as far as the news may have spread throughout, not England only, but France as well; where, as I need not remind you, the most beautiful and durable of monuments has been reared to the genius of Poe, by the laborious devotion of a genius equal and akin to his own; and where the admirable translation of his prose works — by a fellow-poet, whom also we have to lament before his time — is even now being perfected by a careful and exquisite version of his poems, with illustrations full of the subtle and tragic force of fancy which impelled and moulded the original song; a double homage, due to the loyal and loving co-operation of one of the most remarkable younger poets, and one of the most powerful leading painters in France — M. Mallarmé and M. Manes.

It is not for me to offer any tribute here to the fame of your great countryman, or dilate, with superfluous and intrusive admiration, on the special quality of his strong and del·cate genius — so sure of aim, and faultless of touch, in all the better and finer part of work he has left us.

I would only, in conveying to the members of the Poe Memorial Committee my sincere acknowledgment of the honor they have done me in recalling my name on such an occasion, take leave to express my firm conviction that, widely as the fame of Poe has already spread, and deeply as it is already rooted in Europe, it is even now growing wider and striking deeper as time advances; the surest presage that time, the eternal enemy of small and shallow reputations, will prove, in this case also, the constant and trusty friend and keeper of a true poet's full-grown fame.

I remain, dear madam, yours very truly,

A. C. SWINBURNE.

After the conclusion of the letters the following poem, contributed by the well-known dramatic critic and *littérateur*, Mr. William Winter, was read by Miss Rice, with exquisite delicacy and utterance, and received with a burst of applause :

AT POE'S GRAVE.

Cold is the pæan honor sings,
And chill is glory's icy breath,
And pale the garland memory brings
To grace the iron doors of death.

Fame's echoing thunders, long and loud,
  The pomp of pride that decks the pall,
The plaudits of the vacant crowd —
  One word of love is worth them all.

With dews of grief our eyes are dim;
  Ah, let the tear of sorrow start,
And honor, in ourselves and him,
  The great and tender human heart!

Through many a night of want and woe,
  His frenzied spirit wandered wild —
Till kind disaster laid him low,
  And heaven reclaimed its wayward child.

Through many a year his fame has grown, —
  Like midnight, vast, like starlight, sweet. —
Till now his genius fills a throne,
  And nations marvel at his feet.

One meed of justice long delayed,
  One crowning grace his virtues crave: —
Ah, take, thou great and injured shade,
  The love that sanctifies the grave!

God's mercy guard, in peaceful sleep,
  The sacred dust that slumbers here;
And, while around *this tomb we weep*,
  God bless, for us, the mourner's tear!

And may his spirit, hovering nigh,
  Pierce the dense cloud of darkness through,
And know, with fame that cannot die,
  He has the world's affection, too!

The Philharmonic Society then rendered the grand chorus, " He, Watching over Israel," from the "Elijah" of Mendelssohn, with fine effect.

ADDRESS OF PROF. HENRY E. SHEPHERD.

"LADIES AND GENTLEMEN,—It is my purpose to speak of Edgar A. Poe, principally as a poet and as a man of genius. I shall abstain, for the most part, from personal incidents or biographical details. These, though not devoid of interest, pertain properly to the historian of literature or to the biographer. Let his 'strange, eventful history' be reserved for some American Masson, Boswell or Morlen.

"Edgar A. Poe was born in 1809, the birth year of Alfred Tennyson, and of Mrs. Browning, the most gifted poetess of any age. The third great era in English letters had then fairly commenced. The spirit of the elder day was revived; the delusive splendor that had so long gilded the Augustan age of Addison, of Bolingbroke and of Johnson, paled before the marvellous intellectual expansion, the comprehensive culture, that distinguished the first thirty years of the present century; the genius of poesy, no longer circum-

scribed by artificial limits, 1 o longer restrained
by the arbitrary procedures of a reflective age,
ranged in unchecked freedom, reviving the buried
forms of mediæval civilization, the lay of the minstrel, the lyric of the troubadour, the forgotten
splendors of the Arthurian cycle.   One day was
as a thousand years in the growth and development of the human mind.

   "Edgar was in his childhood when our last great
literary epoch had attained the full meridian of
its greatness.   He spent five years at school in
England, from 1816 to 1821.   The term of Edgar's
school life in England was a period of intense
poetic activity and creative form, heroic emprise,
knightly valor, and brilliant achievement.   In
1822, Edgar, then in his fourteenth year, returned
to his native land.   He attained to manhood at a
time when, by a revolution familiar in the history
of every literature, the supremacy was reverting
from poetry to prose.   The cold generalizations
of philosophy chilled the glowing ardor of the
preceding epoch.   The publication of Macaulay's
 Essay on Milton' in 1825 marks the transition
from the sway of the imaginative faculty to the
present unsurpassed period in our prose literature.

From this desultory outline of English literature
during the early years of the poet, you will observe that his intellectual constitution was formed
under peculiar circumstances. He does not belong chronologically to the age of Shelley, Byron
and Keats; his position is one of comparative
isolation, like that of Wyatt, Sackville or Collins, in the midst of an unpoetic generation, un-
sustained by the sweet consolations of poetic
association, or the tender endearments of poetic
sympathy. When he attained to the conscicus-
ness of his great powers, none of those stimulating influences existed, save as matters of history
or poetic tradition. Tennyson in England was
viewing nature in perspective, and involving his
critics in mazes as tangled as the web which
enveloped the fated Lady of Shalott. Wordsworth had abjured the teachings of his early
manhood. Shelley, Keats and Byron were
dead. Morris and Swinburne were yet unborn,
and the thrones of the elder gods were principally
filled by the 'Idle singers of an empty day.'
American poetry had then produced little that
'future ages will not willingly let die.'

POE'S MASTERPIECE.

"Having traced the conditions of the era during which the poet's mind was blooming into maturity, we are now prepared to appreciate the distinctive characteristics of his genius, as revealed in his prose, and especially in his poetry. It is known to students of our literature that in all ages of our literary history, from the time that our speech was reduced to comparative uniformity by the rare perception and philological discrimination of Chaucer, there have existed two recognized schools of poets, the native or domestic, and the classical. In some poets the classical element is the animating principle, as in Milton, whose pages, 'sprinkled with the diamond dust of classic lore,' 'thick as autumnal leaves that strew the brooks in Vallambrosa,' afford the most impressive illustration of its power. A wonderful impulse was communicated to the development of classical poetry, by that 'morning star of modern song,' the poet Keats, and since his advent our poetry has tended, more and more, to divest itself of native sympathies, and to assume an artistic or literary character. Our poetry may have lost pliancy,

but it has gained in elaboration and perfection
of structure. Genius and imagination are not
repressed, but are regulated by the canons of
art, and from their harmonious alliance arises
the unsurpassed excellence of Poe's poetry. In
the school of literary or classical poets he must
be ranked in that illustrious procession which
includes the names of Milton, Ben Jonson, Her-
rick, Shelley and Keats. Having assigned to
Poe an honorable eminence in the school of
classical poets, I proceed to speak of the originality, the creative power, displayed in his poetry,
as well as his brilliant achievements in metrical
combination. Specific points of resemblance
may be discovered between his poetry and that
of his contemporaries or predecessors, but no general or well-defined likeness, and few poets have
displayed a more surpassing measure of creative
power. Some of his maturer poems are almost
without precedent, in form as well as in spirit.
The 'Legend of the Raven,' related by Roger
De Hoveden, and referring to the era of
the Latin conquest of Constantinople, nor the
Legend of Herod Agrippa,' cited by De Quincey in his celebrated 'Essay on Modern Super-

stition,' furnishes an adequate foundation for the text of Poe's masterpiece. The raven has constituted a prominent character in English poetry for many ages. In 'Hamlet,' in 'Macbeth,' in 'Sir David Lindsay,' in Tickell's exquisite ballad of 'Collin and Lucy,' the appearance of this ominous bird of yore will readily suggest itself to all lovers of our dramatic and lyric poetry. But none of these can be considered as the precursor of Poe's 'Raven.' The nearest approach to any distinctive feature of 'The Raven' is to be found, I suspect, in the dramas of Shakspeare, those unfailing sources of intellectual nutriment. The one word, 'Mortimer,' of Harry Percy's 'Starling,' presents a marked phonetic resemblance to the 'Nevermore' of 'The Raven,' whose melancholy refrain seems almost the echo of the 'Starling's' unvarying note. No poem in our language presents a more graceful grouping of metrical appliances and devices. The power of peculiar letters is evolved with a magnificent touch; the thrill of the liquids is a characteristic feature, not only of the refrain, but throughout the compass of the poem, their 'linked sweetness, long drawn out,' falls with a mellow

cadence, revealing the poet's mastery of those
mysterious harmonies which lie at the basis of
human speech. The continuity of the rhythm,
illustrating Milton's ideal of true musical delight,
in which the sense is variously drawn out from
one verse into another, the alliteration of the
Norse minstrel and the Saxon bard, the graphic
delineation and sustained interest, are some of
the features which place 'The Raven' foremost
among the creations of a poetic art in our age
and clime.

"Another distinguishing characteristic of Poe's
poetry is its rhythmical power and its admirable
illustration of that mysterious affinity which binds
together the sound and the sense. Throughout
all the processes of nature, a rhythmical movement is clearly discernible. Upon the conscious
recognition of this principle are based all our
conceptions of melody, all systems of intonation
and inflection. In this dangerous sphere of
poetry, he won a mastery over the properties of
verse that the troubadours might have aspired
to emulate.

CLASSIC ELEMENTS.

"Permit me next to direct your attention to the

classic impress of Poe's poetry, its blending of
genius and culture, and to the estimation in
which his productions are held in other lands.
The Athenian sculptor, in the palmiest days of
Grecian art, wrought out his loveliest conceptions
by the painful processes of unflagging diligence.
The angel was not evolved from the block by a
sudden inspiration or a brilliant flash of unpremeditated art. By proceeding upon a system
corresponding to the diatonic scale in music, the
luxuriance of genius was regulated and directed
by the sober precepts and decorous graces of
formal art. No finer illustration of conscious art
has been produced in our century than 'The
Raven.' In all the riper productions of our
poet, there is displayed the same graceful alliance
of genius, culture and taste. He attained a mastery over the most difficult metrical forms, even
those to whose successful production the spirit
of the English tongue is not congenial. The
sonnet, that peculiarly Italian type of verse
immortalized by the genius of Petrarch, a form
of verse in which few English writers have succeeded, has been admirably illustrated in Poe's
'Zante.' Indeed, much of the acrimony of his

criticism arose from his painful sensitiveness to
artistic imperfection and his enthusiastic worship
of the beautiful. The Grecian cast of his genius
led to a pantheistic love of beauty incarnated in
palpable or material forms. This striving after
sensuous beauty has constituted a distinctive
characteristic of those poets who were most
thoroughly imbued with the Grecian taste and
spirit. It has left its impress deep upon the tex-
ture of our poetry, and many of its most silvery
symphonies owe their inspiration to this source.
In addition to the classic element, his poetry is
pervaded by that magic of style, that strange
unrest and unreality, those weird notes, like the
refrain of his own 'Raven,' 'so musical, so
melancholy,' which are traceable to the Celtic
influence upon our composite intellectual character. The quick sensibility, the ethreal temper
of these natural artists, have wonderfully enlivened the stolid character of our Anglo-Saxon
ancestors, and much of the style and consecutive
power that have reigned in English poetry from
the days of Lajamon, Walter Mapes, and of
Chaucer, may be attributed to the Celtic infusion
into the Teutonic blood. Conspicuous examples

of its power may be discovered in Shakspeare,
in Keats, in Byron and in Poe.

POE'S GENIUS.

" I have thus endeavored to present to you the
intellectual character of Edgar A. Poe as it has
revealed itself to me from the diligent study of
his works, and from many contrasts and coinci-
dences that literary history naturally suggests.
I have attempted to show the versatile character
of his genius, the consummate, as well as conscious, art of his poetry, the graceful blending
of the creative and the critical faculty, — a combination perhaps the rarest that the history of
literature affords, — his want of deference to pro-
totypes or models, the chaste and scholarly elegance of his diction, the Attic smoothness and
the Celtic magic of his style. Much of what he
has written may not preserve its freshness, or
stand the test of critical scrutiny in after-times,
but when subjected to the severest ordeal of vary-
ing fashion, popular caprice, the 'old order
changing, yielding place to new,' there is much
that will perish only with the English language.
The riper productions of Poe have received the

most enthusiastic tributes from the sober and dis-
passionate critics of the Old World. I shall
ever remember the thrill of grateful appreciation
with which I read the splendid eulogium upon
the genius of Poe in 'The London Quarterly
Review,' in which he is ranked far above his
contemporaries, and pronounced one of the most
consummate artists of our era, potentially the
greatest critic that ever lived, and possessing
perhaps the finest ear for rhythm that was ever
formed. You are doubtless familiar with the
impressions produced by 'The Raven' upon the
mind of Mrs. Browning, 'Shakspeare's daughter and Tennyson's sister.' It is but recently
that one of the master spirits of the new poetic
schools has accorded to Poe the pre-eminence
among American poets. Alfred Tennyson has
expressed his admiration, who, with true poetic
ken, was among the first to appreciate the novelty and the delicacy of his method, and who, at
a time when the laureate's fame was obscured by
adverse and undiscerning criticism, plainly fore-
saw the serene splendor of his matured greatness.
An appreciative and generous Englishman has
recently added to the treasures of our literature

a superb edition of his works,* in which ample recognition is accorded to his rare and varied powers, and the slanders of his acrimonious biographer are refuted by evidence that cannot be gainsaid or resisted. No reader of English periodical literature, can fail to observe the frequent allusions to his memory, the numerous tributes to his genius, that have appeared in 'The Athenæum,' 'The Academy,' the British quarterlies, and the translations of the new Shakspeare Society. Nor is this lofty estimate of his poems confined to those lands in which the English language is the vernacular speech; it has extended into foreign climes, and aroused appreciative admiration where English literature is imperfectly known and slightly regared.

"Let us rejoice that Poe's merits have found appropriate recognition, and that the Poets' Corner in our Westminster is rescued from the ungrateful neglect which, for a quarter of a century, has constituted the just reproach of our State and metropolis. I recognize in the dedication of this monument to the memory of our

---

* Edition of Adams and Charles Black, Edinburgh.

poet an omen of highest and noblest import, looking far beyond the mere preservation of his fame by the 'dull, cold marble' which marks his long-neglected grave. The impulse which led to its erection coincides in form and spirit with those grand movements which the zeal and enthusiasm of scholars and patriots in Great Britain and in America have effected within the past ten years for the perpetuation of much that is greatest in the poetry of the English tongue. At last, we have the works of Geoffrey Chaucer restored to their original purity by the praiseworthy diligence of Skeats, Furnival, Child and Bradshaw. At last, we are to add to the golden treasury of our literature genuine editions of Shakspeare, in which the growth of his genius and his art will be traced by the graceful scholarship and penetrating insight of Ingleby, Tennyson, Spedden and Simpson. Ten years have accomplished what centuries failed to achieve, in rescuing from strange and unpardonable indifference the masterpieces of our elder literature, the Sibylline leaves of our ancient poesy. This graceful marble, fit emblem of our poet, is the expression — perhaps unconscious, undesigned,

but none the less effective — of sympathy with
this grand intellectual movement of our era.   I
hail these auspicious omens of the future of our
literature with gratitude and delight.   But while
we welcome these happy indications, while we
rejoice in the critical expansion of our peerless
literature, let us not disregard the solemn injunc-
tion conveyed by this day's proceedings.   While
we pay the last tributes of respect to the memory
of him who alone was worthy, among American
poets, to be ranked in that illustrious procession
of bards around whose names is concentrated
so much of the glory of the English tongue,
from Chaucer to Tennyson, let us cherish the ad-
monition to nurture and stimulate the poetry of
our land, until it ascend, 'with no middle flight,'
into the 'brightest heaven of invention,' and the
regions of purest phantasy."

Professor Shepherd was frequently interrupted
with applause during the delivery of his eloquent
address.   Poe's famous poem of "The Raven"
was then read by Mr. William F. Gill, who was
made the recipient of an ovation at its close, at
the hands of the audience.   The "Inflammatus,"

from Rossini's "Stabat Mater," by Miss Ella
Gordon and the Philharmonic Society, followed.
John H. B. Latrobe, Esq., then gave his interesting personal reminiscences of Poe,* which
were received with peculiar acceptance.

REMARKS OF MR. NEILSON POE.

After Mr. Latrobe had concluded his remarks,
Mr. Neilson Poe, Sr., a cousin of the poet, was
introduced by Prof. Elliott.

Mr. Poe, upon being introduced, said the relatives of the late poet would indeed be wanting
in sensibility, as well as gratitude, if they let
this occasion pass without some acknowledgment
of their special obligation to those who have
reared the memorial soon to be unveiled over
the grave of their kinsman. It is impossible that
they can be indifferent to the increasing fame of
one whose ancestry is common to themselves,
and who share his blood. They cannot but look
with gratification at the fact that the imputations
on the personal character of Poe, which envy

---

* Given in connection with the account of the Baltimore
prizes in our memoir.

has invented and malice magnified, can now, under a closer investigation and an impartial criticism, be judged with charity and justice. Personal animosity may have created slanders which a kindlier spirit is now rejecting, and the good and noble traits of character of the dead, are being recognized by an impartial public.

AT THE GRAVE.

Those present then repaired to Westminster Churchyard, where all that is mortal of Poe reposes. The remains have been removed from their first resting-place, in an obscure corner of the lot, to the corner of Fayette and Greene streets, where the monument now covering the grave can be seen from Fayette street.

While the Philharmonic Society rendered the following dirge, written for the occasion by Mrs. Eleanor Fullerton, of Baltimore, known in the literary world under the pseudonym of "Violet Fuller," the Committee on the Memorial, and others, gathered around the monument.

> Softly sleep, softly sleep,
> Sleep in thy lowly bed,

Sleep, sleep in slumbers deep.
  Waked not by earthly tread.
Over thy grave let the wild winds moan.
Under this fair memorial stone,
Poet, thou slumberest well;
All thy sorrows o'er, sleep for evermore, sleep!

Peace and rest, peace and rest,
  O. weary soul, be thine;
Rest, rest, in earth's cool breast,
  Sheltered from storm and shine.
Darkness no more obscures thy way,
Out of the night, eternal day
Beams forth with power divine.
All thy sorrows o'er, sleep for evermore, sleep!

The dirge is an adaptation of Tennyson's "Sweet and Low," by Mrs. Fullerton. Prof. Elliott and Miss Rice removed the muslin in which the memorial was veiled while the dirge was being sung, and the memorial was then, for the first time, presented to the gaze of the public. The monument was crowned with a wreath composed of ivy, and another of lilies and evergreens. After the dirge, Mr. William F. Gill, of Boston, recited Poe's poem, "Annabel Lee," and Mrs. Dillehunt, a former school teacher, selections from "The Bells." This concluded the exercises, and the throng which had collected in the graveyard came forward to view the monument.

During the exercises a large throng was gathered in the vicinity of Fayette and Greene streets, unable to gain admission to the female high school or the churchyard.

THE MONUMENT.

The monument is of the pedestal form, and is eight feet high; the surbase is of Woodstock granite, and six feet square, the balance being of Italian marble. The pedestal has an Attic base, three feet ten inches square; the die block is a cube three feet square and three feet two inches high, relieved on each face by a square-projecting and polished plane, the upper angles of which are broken and filled with a carved rosette. On the front panel is the bas-relief bust of the poet, modelled by Frederick Volck from a photograph in possession of Mr. Neilson Poe. The other panel contains an inscription of the dates of the birth and death of Poe. The die block is surmounted by a bold and graceful frieze and cornice four feet square, broken on each face, in the centre, by a segment of a cir-

THE MONUMENT ERECTED IN MEMORY OF POE AT BALTIMORE.
NOVEMBER 17TH, 1875.

cle. The frieze is ornamented at the angles by richly carved acanthus leaves, and in the centre by a lyre crowned with laurel. The whole is capped by a blocking three feet square, cut to a low pyramidal form. The monument is simple and chaste, and strikes more by graceful outline, than by crowding with unmeaning ornament. It was designed by Geo. A. Frederick, architect, and built by Col. Hugh Sisson.

A TRIBUTE FROM THE STAGE.

A pleasing feature of the ceremonies was the placing upon the monument of a large wreath of flowers, made up principally of camelias, lilies and tea roses. Together with this, was deposited a floral tribute in the shape of a raven, made from black immortelles. The large petals of the lilies suggested the "bells" immortalized by Poe's genius, the significance of the other emblems being obvious. These were tributes from the company at Ford's Grand Opera House, Mrs. Germon being mainly instrumental in getting them up. Poe's mother had been an actress at Holliday-Street Theatre, which fact had been preserved in the traditions of the stage, and had something to do with inspiring this tribute.

MEMORIAL SUGGESTIONS.

The inscriptions upon the monument have yet (1875) to be determined upon. Various suggestions have been received, among them that from the poet Longfellow, read as a portion of the exercises. Oliver Wendell Holmes has suggested the following, taken from Poe's verses, "To one in Paradise : "

> "Ah, dream too bright to last —
> Ah, starry hope that didst arise
> But to be overcast."

James Russell Lowell, in a letter to Miss Rice, has recommended that some passage from Poe's works be selected, in allusion to the self-caused wretchedness of his life, and suggests the stanza of "The Raven" beginning, "An unhappy master," &c., to the end of the verse. Together with this, he recommends a selection expressing the peculiar musical quality of Poe's genius, and suggests a verse of the "Haunted Palace," beginning, "And all with pearl and ruby glowing."

In response to a letter of inquiry, the venerable poet Bryant furnishes the following as a suitable inscription : —

TO
EDGAR ALLAN POE
Author of the Raven
And other poems,
And of various works of fiction,
Distinguished alike
For originality in the conception,
Skill in word painting,
And power over the mind of the reader,
The Public School Teachers
Of Baltimore,
Admirers of his genius,
Have erected this monument.